Severance

A Hardlands Prelude

Joss G. Hamilton

SEVERANCE *A Hardlands Prelude*

Published by GW Scribbles Australia

First Edition: 2026

ISBN: 978-1-7642318-7-9

Cover design by GW Scribbles

DEDICATION

To my beloved wife, whose steady presence during late-night writing sessions mirrors the quiet competence of those who keep essential systems running when the world grows uncertain.

To my goddaughters, especially Kailana, whose bright enthusiasm for engineering and problem-solving inspired a fictional namesake who refuses to let cities fall dark. May your generation inherit the courage to choose work over theatre, and the wisdom to know that the most important battles are won with steady hands rather than grand gestures.

To my dear friend Gregory, whose proud stories about Kailana's enrollment at UQ sparked the ember that became Lieutenant Reyes' unwavering determination. Your belief in the next generation's capability echoes in every page where competence triumphs over chaos.

To the engineers, emergency responders, and quiet professionals who keep the lights on and the water flowing—may this story honor the unglamorous work that makes civilization possible.

And to those who dream of an Australia that stands firm in an uncertain world, may these twenty-four hours offer a glimpse of the resilience that lies dormant until the moment it's desperately needed.

CONTENTS

ACKNOWLEDGMENTS

Severance emerged from a fascination with how ordinary people respond to extraordinary circumstances, and how middle-power nations like Australia might navigate a world where the old rules no longer apply. This radio-play styled novella represents both homage to classic dramatic broadcasts like Orson Welles' *War of the Worlds* and a love letter to the television series *24*—exploring how crisis unfolds in real time, hour by hour, decision by decision.

The technical authenticity woven throughout these pages owes much to extensive research into Australian Defence Force procedures, military terminology, and the intersection of Australian and American strategic interests. While I claim no military expertise, I strived to capture the authentic voice of professionals who serve with quiet competence rather than theatrical heroism.

Special recognition must go to Claude from Anthropic, whose editorial collaboration helped refine character voices, technical accuracy, and the complex choreography of a twenty-four-hour crisis. Our work together exemplified the story's central theme—that the most important victories are won through careful attention to detail rather than dramatic gestures.

To my friend Gregory, whose proud sharing of his daughter's engineering journey provided the inspiration for Lieutenant Kailana Reyes. Your stories of a young woman choosing technical challenges over easier paths reminded me that heroes often wear hi-vis vests rather than capes.

The geographical settings—from Darwin's industrial pragmatism to Williamtown's quiet professionalism, from Newcastle's resilient infrastructure to the broader Hunter Valley's understated strength—reflect personal connections to places where real people do essential work without fanfare.

To the early readers who understood that this novella serves as a gateway to the larger *Hardlands* universe, thank you for recognizing that Australia's story in an uncertain world deserves telling from an Australian perspective. Your encouragement affirmed that middle-power nations have voices worth hearing in discussions of global change.

Finally, to the next generation of engineers, service members, journalists, and citizens who will inherit the world these characters defend—may you find in their example the courage to choose competence over performance, community over chaos, and the patient work of preservation over the easy temptation of destruction.

The hardest lands often produce the strongest foundations. This is just the beginning of that story.

CHAPTER 1: HOUR 00:00
FIRST CUT

Lieutenant Kailana Reyes

The graphs should have been flat—midnight in Darwin was supposed to be boring. Midnight in Darwin was supposed to be a flat line: the HVDC hum from the desert substation, optical repeaters thumping like a slow heart somewhere under a thousand kilometers of black water. But on Kailana Reyes' screen the trace was jagged—alive—like something was sawing at the artery itself.

"No." She rolled her chair closer.

The wall display threw pale light across the empty control room: cable map left, grid telemetry center, intrusion detection right. The air-conditioning hissed. Somewhere beyond the cyclone shutters, mangroves breathed with the tide. She zoomed the event log until timestamps filled the screen.

00:00:13 — PTP drift detected (8.6 µs) on Segment SGP-DWN03. 00:00:22 — Attenuation spike (+4.2 dB) repeater R-337. 00:00:31 — Transient undervoltage HVDC link C-NT02—Protection armed (Stage 1).

Something had reached up through the Timor Sea and put a finger on their throat.

Her hands found the keyboard. She isolated SGP-DWN03, ran

an OTDR trace—optical time-domain reflectometry spinning out like sonar. A clean line would return like a bell. This one came back ragged, then flat, then a pattern of teeth where there shouldn't be any.

Cut. Not a blunt break. Deliberate.

She pushed a whisper of commands through the out-of-band management tunnel to R-337. The repeater coughed a reply in machine pidgin, then went silent mid-handshake.

The silence felt intentional.

00:01:12 — *BGP route withdrawal observed—APAC IX.*

Not just here. Somewhere an exchange was being torn apart in the dark. She flicked to the IDS panel. Green, green, green—then: *Would you like to allow firmware update for vendor capsule?* Six months old, signed correctly. She'd personally told the system to ignore correctly signed updates at midnight.

She hard-blocked it. The request returned with a new certificate, valid from ten minutes in the future.

"Cute." She smiled cold and small.

The red phone—actual plastic, a relic that bypassed the internet—sat at her elbow. She lifted it.

"Darwin Defence Comms, Reyes."

The night watch petty officer answered on the second ring. "Ma'am?"

"Raise Joint Defence Northern Command. General Monash's operations desk. We have a likely physical event on SunCable, Singapore link. Confirmed anomalies at R-337 and SGP-DWN03. Spoofed firmware updates on out-of-band. Not a test."

Chair creak. "Copy. Routing you."

She was already typing. The HVDC panel complained, the bar

graph dipping. The inverter yard south of town would be ringing like a cathedral. She told the system to prepare soft islanding if the line continued to sag. Hospitals first. Then water, then base, then everything else.

The red phone clicked alive. Gravel voice, baked by the NT sun.

"Monash."

"Lieutenant Kailana Reyes, Defence Communications, sir. We've got a cut. Not clean—looks like an ROV's taken bites out of the segment toward Singapore. Out-of-band management being hit with spoofed updates. HVDC seeing staged undervoltage. I'm prepping islanding."

"How sure?"

She looked at the trace. The teeth looked back. "Eighty-five percent. Going to ninety if my OTDR returns the same."

"Assume ninety. I'm bringing a team online. Any other anomalies?"

"BGP withdrawals at APAC exchange. Certificate time-skew. PTP drift. It's coordinated—midnight, low staffing, low load."

"Raise the hospital. Warn them. Keep your islanding hand off the switch until you must. I'd prefer power now and blackness later to a flatline in theatre. Get Canberra on secure. Keep talking to me."

"Yes, sir."

The line clicked dead.

She dialled the hospital on copper that had outlived digital dreams. The supervisor answered fast. "You may see unstable mains. Stand up all generators. Treat this like a cyclone without rain."

"How bad?" the nurse asked. Three NICU mothers were already pacing the corridor.

"Bad enough to prepare."

00:07:04 — *OTDR return (path B): fault located at 23.6 km from Head A; secondary attenuation 47.2 km.*

Two bites, placed precisely. Someone had marked this cable weeks ago.

She pinged Noah Tan on the internal roster—night shift at the port, the kind of engineer who printed crosswords on continuous feed. His camera showed stubble and concern.

"AIS is weird," he said before she could ask. Ships broadcasting as dashes or playing the same recording on loop. "Like someone recorded a fishing fleet."

"Screenshot everything. If you see anything that flies or crawls under a false flag, you run."

"Understood." Then softer: "Call your sister. Before the phones decide they don't love you."

She opened the islanding panel and dragged power districts with two fingers. Royal Darwin Hospital: Priority 1. Desal: Priority 2. Air base: Priority 3A. Everywhere else shuffled back. She set trip points and wrote a note to herself to lower them if needed.

00:12:19 — *HVDC link C-NT02: Undervoltage sustained (Stage 2). Protection armed.*

"Come on," she said to the sea, to whatever was down there with lights and manipulators. "Show me where you're going next."

The intrusion detection offered a gift: *New session request: vendor capsule—high priority.* Right MAC, right nonce, right signature. Uncanny politeness.

It knew what she knew.

She unplugged the management uplink and set it aside, then walked the cable to a dead-end switch she kept for days like this. The switch booped cheerful ignorance.

The red phone rang.

"Reyes."

"Monash. Canberra's slow. I'm seeing ghosts on radar. Could be weather. Could be someone drawing fairy lights. JORN's reporting slight anomalies too."

JORN—the over-the-horizon radar could see things take off two countries away. "Slight anomalies" meant someone was masking or multiplying.

"I'm not losing the room to them. Hard-blocked management updates. HVDC arming Stage Two. Two physical events on Singapore segment."

"I will need the island if this continues."

"You'll have it."

He hung up. She swore softly and checked the hospital line. Generators standing, NICU steady. They asked if this was China. She said attribution belonged to people with portfolios—her job was keeping lights on.

Then the IDS pulsed different.

00:18:04 — *Privileged credentials observed (DAR-CBR NAT), origin: Parliament House / Secure.*

Internal Canberra traffic stepping through an authorised NAT, wanting read access to repeater configurations. Valid key from someone who should never need to touch a repeater.

She opened the metadata like a surgeon. The deputy National Security Advisor's office. Data path neat as an assassin's handwriting.

She didn't approve it. She didn't reject it. She caged it in a VM and watched it scratch.

Outside, something thumped. Not explosion—a bin rolled by

wind. Her muscles clenched anyway. On the map the hospital district held at 49.7 Hz.

00:23:39 — *OTDR return (path C): third attenuation at 71.0 km.*

Three bites. Deliberate.

She wrote the first SITREP on paper:

SITREP 00:24Z+10 SunCable SGP-DWN03 experiencing multiple mechanical attenuations consistent with hostile ROV activity. HVDC link arming Stage 2. IDS reports multiple spoofed vendor capsules, blocked. BGP instability at APAC IX. PTP drift observed. AIS anomalies near Darwin approaches. — Lt. K. Reyes, ADF Defence Comms (Darwin)

She printed it to dead tree. Paper didn't reboot.

The lights flickered. Once. Twice.

00:26:01 — *HVDC link C-NT02: Undervoltage sustained (Stage 3). Protection DISARMED (override).*

"Hey—" She pulled up trip points, lowered them by 0.05 Hz. The graph wobbled, found a new line.

The Canberra request reshaped itself with different credentials. Same office. Someone important was impatient.

She tagged it: *Queued for peer review; Darwin link unstable; local authority retains change control until grid stabilizes.* She signed her name and rank. If they wanted to arrest someone later, they'd know exactly who.

The air-conditioning took a softer breath. The world could be quiet and enormous right before it broke.

00:31:44 — *Unauthorized console login attempt—blocked (five).*
00:31:45 — *Unauthorized console login attempt—blocked (six).*

She yanked the keyboard out entirely, wired in a hardware kill through a tiny serial line. If software wanted to seduce you, hardware was indifferent.

Her phone buzzed. Unknown number: *Approve update. It will help stability.*

"Send cake," she typed back.

No answer.

The hospital blinked—quick check. NICU stable. She sent a thumbs-up and hated herself for using emoji in what might be war.

She looked at the wall map and let herself see the shape: undersea cable cut in three places, exchange routes withdrawn, time tilted, a fleet that might be lying, radar seeing too much or nothing, someone with Parliament keys sweet-talking the management plane. Midnight start. No manifesto. Just screws turning.

A trap. Twenty-four hours of cascading failures designed to make good people choose between wrong and less wrong.

00:39:02 — *Alarm: Temperatures rising at Relay Yard Δ2.*

That was here. She called security. The guard smelled metal. She vented the yard, shut down inverters before cascade.

00:43:17 — *OTDR return (path D): attenuation at 71.0 km increased by 3.1 dB.*

They'd come back to lean on the third bite.

The red phone rang.

"Reyes."

"Monash. Canberra's half awake. We're seeing noise over the Arafura. If I tell you to island the hospital and base, let the rest go dark—can you do that without the grid sulking?"

"Yes. On your call. Someone's trying to come through our management from Parliament House."

He cursed once, softly. "Hold them in the box."

"Yes, sir."

"Good work."

The praise hit unexpected. She put it aside.

00:52:09 — *JORN alert (summary): low-RCS contacts intermittently observed; possible autonomous aerial vehicles; confidence LOW-MED.*

LOW-MED from conservative JORN meant the math was leaning one way.

The building shuddered.

A dull sound, not close. The guard's voice on intercom: "Ma'am? Lights out toward the bay. Not a chopper."

Her heart did something precise and unpleasant. "Inside. Now. Lock the door."

00:57:33 — *Hospital mains failure—generator engaged.*

The NICU square blinked from GRID to GEN. Somewhere nurses in soft shoes watched monitors instead of faces.

"Okay," she said to the room. "We're up."

EYES-ONLY: *JORN classifies swarm signatures trending south. Confidence MEDIUM. Recommend air intercept readiness east coast.*

She pulled the islanding lever.

The control room lights dimmed to emergency.

In the dark, something was moving.

CHAPTER 2: HOUR 01:00
THE WEIGHT ARRIVES

Prime Minister Patricia Keating

The phone on Patricia Keating's nightstand didn't ring so much as insist—a vibration that carried weight. She was already reaching when she answered.

"Keating."

"Prime Minister, apologies." Kira Patel, duty secretary, voice crisp with controlled alarm. "Northern grid fluctuations, undersea comms irregularities on the Singapore link, isolated banking outages. Defence requests you in the Situation Room."

"How isolated?"

"Darwin first, now spreading. IDS holding for now. Time-protocol drift and spoofed vendor updates. APAC exchange withdrawals."

"Call the Defence Minister, Home Affairs, Treasurer. Keep Foreign on a short leash—no ambassador calls yet. Wake my husband, tell him I'll text when I can."

"Yes, Prime Minister."

Keating stood in the dark, felt the weight arrive. She dressed fast—dark trousers, white shirt—and moved through the silent apartment. The corridor lights made Canberra look like an abandoned set. In the elevator mirror, she saw the face people called when they couldn't say crisis yet.

The Situation Room wasn't a bunker but a den with better screens. Inside, three panes split the main display: **GRID**, **CABLE**, **COMMS**. A fourth showed a world map with embassy markers like quiet accusations.

Defence Minister Peter Hastings arrived through the opposite door, jacket over pajamas, tie in pocket. They nodded—a concession that screens were in charge for now.

"Report," Keating said.

Chief of Staff Marta Vale handled the handoff with surgical precision. "Midnight saw SunCable events. Darwin's Lieutenant Reyes has isolated three attenuations on the Singapore segment—hostile ROV activity. HVDC link arming protections. IDS blocking spoofed vendor updates with clean signatures and wrong clocks."

"Banking?"

"Tentative outages spreading from Darwin. Treasury's not panicking yet."

"Radar?" Hastings's voice dropped like ordnance.

"JORN seeing anomalies. Low-to-medium confidence. Civil aviation feeds are noise."

"And overseas?" Keating's eyes on the world map. "Tell me this isn't just us."

"APAC IX spitting route withdrawals. Chatter of embassy protests in Jakarta and Manila—unconfirmed."

Keating assembled the shape in her mind. Midnight start. Low staffing. A pattern woven across water, power, time. She took the head of the table without ceremony.

"Frames. We assign frames. Marta—Grid and Cable. Peter—Defence, including air readiness north and east. Kira—Home

Affairs, police posture, hospitals. I'll hold Foreign, Treasury, and the public line. We don't guess out loud. We don't brief with adjectives. We don't use the word war."

Hastings's jaw clicked. "Rules of engagement?"

"Defensive. We won't escalate on ghosts. But if you need to keep people breathing, do what you must. I'll carry it."

Defence Space Command joined the bridge—a colonel in WA, backlit by antenna schematics. "We're seeing elevated noise on LEO links. Nothing we can't ride. We've moved select nodes to priority blackout protocols to preserve space-domain integrity if terrestrial fails."

"Commercial partnerships remain viable if needed."

"Thank you. Hold those decisions at colonel level. Ministerial cover if required."

Hastings shot her a look. She gave him one back: later.

"Where are we on undersea?"

"Lieutenant Reyes prepping controlled islanding. Hospital, water, base prioritized. Her read is deliberate—three bites, not random."

"And who's holding the knife?" Hastings's way of not saying China.

"Attribution lives downstream of evidence."

"Patricia—"

"Peter."

The door opened. Marcus Reid slipped in, tie perfect, hair perfect, the kind of perfect that looked rehearsed. He took a chair with practiced ease.

"Catching up. Vendor capsules spoofed? Novel. We should push an emergency patch."

"From here?" Keating knew the answer.

"Parliament has secure keys—"

"Leave the keys in your pocket. We don't touch repeaters from this building while Darwin's on fire control."

Reid smiled as if she'd made a joke. She filed the feeling.

Kira slipped a note: **Hospitals standing generators. NICU stable.**

"We're raising National Security Posture to Amber. Defence at Condition Two North, Three East. Air ready NT, intercept readiness Williamtown if JORN confidence climbs. Home Affairs brings AFP and States to readiness—riot control quiet. Treasury preps a statement: technical outages, redundancy in place. Foreign drafts lines to Jakarta and Manila: monitoring, friends, counsel calm."

"And the public?"

"Nothing until we understand more. Speaking too soon shapes panic. Too late, we become the panic."

Hastings looked at Defence Space Command. "If civil comms degrade—"

"Redundancies exist. We'll keep secure voice. There are other paths if needed." The colonel's non-answer carried weight.

Keating caught the look, held it, let it go. Tonight wasn't for shopping allies.

Darwin came up on audio. Lieutenant Reyes, clear and contained: "Three discrete attenuations on SGP-DWN03, consistent with ROV interference. HVDC armed Stage Two. Intrusion attempts on management plane from Parliament House NAT are boxed. Recommend no remote pushes."

Silence clean enough to hear lies slide. Keating didn't look at Reid.

"Good work, Lieutenant. Your recommendation accepted. You're authorized to island on General Monash's call combined with yours."

"Yes, Prime Minister."

Vale's pen scratched. "We'll audit the NAT logs."

"After sunrise. Until then, nobody moves without fingerprints in ink."

Hastings's phone lit. He threw the feed to the wall—grainy handheld video from Jakarta. A crowd outside the embassy compound. Placards, fire. The metadata anyone's guess.

"Unverified," Vale said immediately.

"Verified enough for an extra ring on the embassy."

"Do it discreetly. If it's staged, we don't supply extras."

Her phone buzzed. Her husband: *Tea on the bench. Proud of you. As always.* She let it warm the place she didn't show the room.

The Jakarta desk answered on the third ring. "There are agitators in the street. Police present. If someone wanted a photograph suggesting crisis, they could have it in five minutes."

"And do they?"

"They do. We expect more."

"Shelter our people. Don't feed the theatre."

"Understood, Prime Minister."

Hastings tapped the table. "If JORN confidence climbs, Williamtown needs a green light. East coast will be target-rich at dawn."

"Condition Three East. Not Two. Not yet."

He wanted to argue. He didn't. One reason she kept him.

Reid cleared his throat. "Prime Minister, the Combined Space

Operations agreements allow for—"

"Tonight we practice not touching anything we don't have to."

He smiled. Storm-smile. She pictured throwing it down stairs.

The COMMS pane hiccupped—static, recovery. The room's breath synced with the screens.

"JORN update. Confidence rising. LOW to MED."

"Williamtown to ready-two. No scramble yet."

Kira slid paper: **AFP reports crowd at ABC Sydney. Social feeds volatile.**

"We'll need to speak publicly before dawn."

"Yes. On analog. On channels that can't be pushed offline."

Defence Space Command's colonel inclined his head. "We're preserving the right orbits. Our commercial partners are aware but not engaged."

The clock read 01:26.

"Peter, call Monash. Tell him he has my cover to island when he must. If he needs to disobey peacetime procedure, he will and I'll sign after."

Hastings smiled—flash of teeth. "With pleasure."

"Marcus, you sit in this room and don't touch a keyboard until Marta's team has clean chain of custody for anything you propose."

He held up both hands. "Of course."

"Then let's begin. We're not a headline tomorrow. We're a country tonight."

FOREIGN rang back. "Jakarta?"

"Prime Minister. Local fiber died mid-call. Failing to backup. Crowd larger. We're sheltering."

"Stay interior. Don't engage."

The line went from green to amber to patient red.

The world map zoomed without being asked, showing the Pacific like a lung.

"Treasury reports U.S. exchanges unavailable. Could be maintenance. Could be—"

"Could be," Keating cut the speculation. "We deal with our hour."

She felt the country on the other end of the wires. All the quiet rooms where people had no word for geopolitics but would carry its weight.

"Record. Prime Minister Patricia Keating. National Security Posture Amber. Defence Conditions Two North, Three East. Air ready-two Williamtown. Hospitals sustained on generator north. Grid islanding on commander plus engineer authority. No attribution, no speculation, no adjectives. We are steady. We are awake."

She paused for breath, not effect.

"And if this is a test, we will fail it slowly, together, until we find the part that breaks the test."

On the wall: **APAC IX: further withdrawals — SE Asia**.

Hastings swore softly.

Keating didn't. She let the next hour arrive and stood to meet it.

CHAPTER 3: HOUR 02:00 NORTHERN EYES

Major General Michael Monash

The ops floor at Northern Command never slept; it dozed with one eye open. Fluorescent light, filtered air, the mild terror of a room designed to notice everything wrong. Michael Monash stepped in with coffee he didn't want and a pen he did, nodded to the watchkeepers, and took position behind the horseshoe of screens.

"Sir," Wing Commander Julia Ng said without standing—movement was currency here. "SunCable's dirty. Three attenuations toward Singapore. Lieutenant Reyes recommends islanding on your authority if HVDC drops."

"I've spoken to her. We hold as long as possible. What's JORN?"

Ng flicked a window. "Low-RCS contacts intermittent, Arafura sector, trending south. Confidence building."

Flight Lieutenant Hargreaves raised a hand from the back. "Civil radar's scrambled, sir. If someone's playing with time protocols, they're playing hard."

"Understood. Security state?"

"Amber. Base access tightened. Armed patrols up. NORFORCE notified—coastline eyes deployed."

"NORFORCE sees what satellites can't." Monash set the coffee down—duty, not pleasure. "Get me Border Force sitrep. I want AIS anomalies catalogued. And let's look at anything calling itself a fishing fleet."

Ng's fingers were already moving. On the wall, the northern approaches showed blue polygons moving across water. Too regular. Too perfect. The sea loved liars.

He picked up the secure handset. "Reyes."

"Sir," her voice steady, the kind that made others calm without knowing why. "HVDC armed Stage Two and holding. Repeaters on SGP-DWN03 being picked like a lock, not smashed. We've boxed spoofed vendor capsules. And we've got management traffic from Parliament House NAT."

"Noted. My authority plus yours to island when required. Hospital first. Then desal, base. Everyone else waits. If you have to choose between tidy and alive—"

"Alive. Yes, sir."

"Good." He cut the line and looked at Ng. "Parliament's NAT pointing fingers?"

"Logged and quarantined. I've asked Canberra for a list of key holders."

"They'll send us poetry. We'll read it at dawn."

Hargreaves cleared his throat. "Sir, AIS is performing ballet. Some tracks are perfect. Humans are messy—"

"Mark perfect behavior as suspect."

The phone rang. NORFORCE Patrol Three, an elder's voice from the Cobourg coast. "General, lights running quiet northeast. No sound until close. Then a hum like a fridge."

"Distance?"

"Hard to judge. They blink like they're thinking."

"Keep distance. Report, don't intercept. You're eyes, not heroes."

"Copy."

Ng's console pinged. "Border Force. ADV Cape Byron reports silent AIS triangles east of Bathurst Island. Nothing close enough to greet."

"No tag games. Watch and note."

He pulled the pen cap off with his teeth and wrote three words on his pad: **Protect. Preserve. Prove.** Protect life. Preserve capability. Prove attribution later.

ASD came up on screen—a civilian with shadows under his eyes. "Sir, complex capsule spoofing across operational tech. Clean certs, wrong clocks. BGP withdrawals APAC-wide—some panic, some planned. Minimize remote management."

"Already done. Tell Parliament to keep their fingers out."

The civilian coughed. "We're discussing that at speed."

"Discuss faster."

He looked at the air picture. Faint returns ghosting. Low observables that might be weather, might be plastic with batteries and purpose.

"Sir," Hargreaves said, voice settling. "If those are drones, they're small, quiet, flying smart."

"Prep ROE for drones. We're not in peacetime doctrine—we're in protect-the-living doctrine."

Ng slid him a sitrep. **Hospitals on generator. Desal ready.** Reyes had printed her life and was living it. He liked her without having properly met her.

"Sir," the domestic desk major said, "AFP reports crowd forming at ABC Sydney. Small, noisy."

"Tell them gentle. We're running a fever—don't add bruises."

He took the handset for Canberra. "Prime Minister."

Keating answered immediately, as if holding the phone. "Michael."

"Ma'am, my posture: Security Amber Darwin and Tindal. NORFORCE eyes out. Border Force tracking AIS anomalies. JORN shows low-RCS trending south, confidence rising. East coast at ready-two. If I have to island in thirty, I will."

"You have my cover. Keep rhetoric cold. No adjectives, no enemies until we can point at something that bleeds."

"Understood."

"And Michael—protect your people first. We can rebuild cables."

"Yes, Prime Minister."

He hung up. The pen rolled once between his fingers—his father's trick for looking calm while thinking sharp.

The secure handset buzzed with an unexpected caller ID—Western Australia, but not military. He let it go to holding. Whatever Woomera's commercial partners wanted could wait.

"Julia, issue local air defence rules—low-slow drones near fuel or ammo, we light them. Shotguns if necessary."

"Yes, sir. Darwin EOD and fire crews on short leash."

A comms tech pointed at a panel, voice pitched high. "Sir, tactical air picture unstable—latency spikes, then blanks."

"When a picture lies, go to windows." To Hargreaves: "Your audio?"

"Too clean. Someone wants us hearing lullabies."

NORFORCE called again. Different voice, younger, excited despite himself. "Boss, Patrol Seven. Wakes off Melville. They roll like snakes, not props."

"Stay back and alive. Thermal if safe, otherwise just eyes."

The relay yard went amber—temperature rising. Reyes was already venting. If you anthropomorphized machines, they behaved. Or you behaved.

"Reyes. You still there?"

"Always. If you ask me to juggle more—"

"Keep the pumps arrogant."

Hargreaves's set peeped. "Sir, I'm getting scatter suggesting fewer toys. Either running out or saving for the next party."

"Or they've done what they came to do," Ng said.

The room's lighting dipped slightly. Five heads turned.

"HVDC flicker, Stage Two holding. Reyes is riding it."

He felt pride for someone he knew only as a voice and competence.

"All right. Attention to air picture."

Hargreaves squinted at his console. "This is eccentric. Picture, not-picture, then Christmas card."

"Pick one to hate."

"I hate the Christmas card."

Ng's phone lit. "Cape Byron being shadowed by something with no radar return, no AIS. But there's a wake."

"Tell them continue as if not being watched."

The air picture blinked. Once. Twice. Fragments like a jigsaw.

Then black.

Not the room—just the air. Every input that made sky make sense went for a smoke.

"Is this us?" Monash asked, knowing.

"No," Hargreaves said. "This is them."

"How long?"

"However long they want."

Monash looked at the clock: 02:37. Someone had blinded them. That left the third option from Duntroon's wall: **Act.**

"Right. Lost the pretty picture but not lost. Julia—shorten loops. Five-minute reporting cadence. NORFORCE keeps eyes. Border Force maintains distance. EOD and fire ready on my word. Reyes—treat your grid like a patient in shock."

"Sir," Ng said, everyone watching him. "Rules if picture doesn't return?"

"If you see a thing wanting to be a weapon, you make it not a thing."

The clock clicked toward 03:00. Outside, objects moved through air that refused to tell him. They would learn to hear with different organs.

CHAPTER 4: HOUR 03:00 PERFECT COPIES

Noah Tan

The port after midnight was a machine that dreamed. Cranes stood like sleeping animals, container stacks in neat teeth, the channel lights pulsing toward black water. In the systems room at East Arm, Noah Tan watched the port's heartbeat scroll across three mismatched monitors and knew something was dying.

The customs gateway threw an error that shouldn't exist. Green tick to amber to green to amber. The status string said **RECONCILE**—a word the gateway didn't know.

He checked the time server. The PTP graph wasn't a slope but a staircase, each step ten microseconds of lie. The AIS feed ticked like a metronome, but when he clicked any triangle, the transponder details came back as dashes or perfect copies of perfect copies.

He printed the screen to an offline box. Old habits save you when clever ones kill you. The cheap thermal paper went into a ring folder already thick with the night's anomalies.

His phone buzzed. Kailana Reyes.

K. Reyes: *You seeing port-side AIS loops?* **Noah:** *Like a choir lip-syncing.* **K. Reyes:** *Border Force watching. Hospital to gen. Hold your ground.*

On Camera 12, three shapes moved through the sodium light. Hi-vis vests, new and wrong. The men inside walked like they knew the layout but not the names.

Camera 7 showed one kneeling at Fiber Pit 7, gloved hands on the metal lid. He had the calm of rehearsal.

Noah grabbed the radio. "Aroha, you near Pit 7?"

Aroha Te Wera—night guard, ex-ADF—came back low. "West side. Why?"

"Three blokes with fresh vests making friends with my fiber."

"I can introduce myself."

"From distance. I'm not paying for heroics."

He watched them lift the lid with practiced grace. One dropped something in—a can, black-taped, Coke-sized. They replaced the lid and walked away without looking up. They knew about cameras and didn't care.

Noah stood. The door had a bolt he'd requested and a steel bar he'd made. Both slid into place.

On the terminal operating system rack, an LED went from normal blink to irritated strobe. **UPDATE**. A window popped:

Apply safety patch to crane controllers? Vendor capsule validated. Urgent.

He unplugged the management ethernet and dropped it in his shirt pocket. The window stayed up and revalidated itself against nothing.

He grabbed his old laptop—no Wi-Fi, no faith—and talked to the switch through serial. The switch purred truth. He hid the update behind other windows.

Shadow at the window. Another. Aroha on security channel: "Police coming. I gave your lads a nice hello from twenty meters. They suggested I mind my business."

"And?"

"I suggested business was my business."

The management console tried again: **Approve vendor capsule? Improves stability.** The cursor moved by itself, then stuttered.

"Send cake," he said, and pulled the plug.

The building sighed. Lights dimmed, recovered, dimmed again. On the wall monitor, Warehouse C showed a four-rotor drone zipping along rafters. It dropped something onto an electrical cabinet. Sparks, then dark.

"Party favors," someone said behind him. Ari, the night forklift driver, had appeared with Aroha.

"Fire crew?" Aroha asked the radio. It repeated her request back in a voice that wasn't hers. She sprinted for the extinguisher rack.

Noah dialed the copper fire line. It rang forever. "Drone. Sparks. Cabinet in C."

"On it."

The update window returned with a certificate that was impossible—valid, signed, perfect, and wrong.

He wrote on a Post-it: **Parliament NAT?** and stuck it where he'd hate it later.

Footsteps in the corridor. A man in virgin hi-vis filled the doorway, holding a lanyard like a talisman. "Systems check. Control sent us."

"Which control?"

"The main one."

Noah reached for the steel bar. "Close the door behind you."

The man didn't. He took a step in. A second man loomed behind, heavier hands.

Aroha appeared with a CO_2 extinguisher over one shoulder. "Boys. Uniform's wrong. Boots are wrong. That lanyard might as well say Bunnings."

The first man laughed—wrong choice. Aroha put the extinguisher nozzle on his sternum with a soft *shh* that made questions. "Door. Bar."

Noah barred it. The second man rattled from outside and discovered walls.

"Police in two," Aroha said. "We can be good until then."

The lights went brown. The UPS grunted. Somewhere a generator coughed alive.

The terminal system went to **FAILSAFE**. Cameras greyed, then black. AIS became dashes. The panel said **MAINS** gone, **GEN** unhappy but present.

A thud—not explosion, not yet—came from the fuel farms. Weight with intent. The door vibrated as the men tried shouldering through steel. Aroha tapped the nozzle against it gently.

Noah's phone buzzed.

K. Reyes: *We lost mains to hospital. Holding on gen. You?* **Noah:** *Blackout. Intrusions. Fire in C.* **K. Reyes:** *Tell Monash. Hang on.*

Blue lights strobed off containers. The men at the door evaporated.

"Society," Aroha said.

The generator hiccupped, steadied. Out on the channel, something moved in the water—not a boat. Like a line drawn with a finger.

On his screen, a new message appeared where it shouldn't:

JORN: Low-RCS contacts, confidence raising. Trend south. Another: **Hold. Do not announce.**

His phone buzzed. Unknown number: *Approve update. It will help stability.*

He typed what Reyes had taught him: *Send cake.*

This time a reply: *Soon.*

A police knock—actual knuckles. "Port Security? Police."

Aroha lifted the bar.

The hallway was lit blue and white. For a second, peace.

Then the sky over the harbour tore into sound that wasn't thunder. The fuel farms camera went white then black. The floor moved half a centimeter and remembered.

The UPS screamed.

"Okay," Noah said to the room, to the port, to the night that had stopped dreaming. "We're up."

The lights went out. Only the little **GEN** square stayed green and patient as the hour balanced on the edge of war.

CHAPTER 5: HOUR 04:00 COMMA TELL

Sophie Kerr

The newsroom screens lied to her.

They said the world was still there, just buffering. Feeds froze mid-frame. A presenter in Melbourne held a smile for twelve seconds before her face turned into polite squares. On the assignment board, pins glowed for Jakarta, Manila, Darwin, Canberra. The wall clock clicked to 04:00 with metronome confidence.

Sophie Kerr set her coffee on paper that used to be a rundown. The mug didn't leave a ring—the coffee had gone cold an hour ago. She pulled her notebook from her back pocket and wrote:

Power flicker north

Cable bites

Our job: oxygen

Behind glass, Master Control looked like men who'd decided tonight was the night. Marty O'Hagan, senior transmission engineer, lifted his chin from patch cables and gave a two-finger salute: *We're here.* He held up a sign—**AM Fallback if we go dumb**—then turned back to panels that had survived more governments than she had.

"Anything on wires?" she asked Zed—Zehra Idris, junior

producer with piano-wire spine.

"AP, Reuters, AFP all saying 'developing situation.' Which means they know nothing."

"Call Jakarta direct. Manila. Anyone not invoicing through platforms having nervous breakdowns."

The social wall scrolled its disease. #ItWasAnAccident, #TurnItBackOn, #SunCableSabotage. A video of three men at a port fence, tagged Darwin. Embassy crowds, tagged Jakarta. A Bankstown petrol station taking cash only, tagged Sydney, looping into punchline.

Sophie's phone buzzed. Unknown number.

I have footage from inside Parliament. Keys. NAT.

She thumbed back: *No cash. Email or drop, no malware.*

You'll want this.

She sent an isolated inbox address: *Try a payload, I'll name you live.*

Three dots. Then nothing.

Zed, hand over ear: "Jakarta stringer says embassy mobilization is organized. Printed placards, not handwritten. Police present and bored. Can't send pictures—deliberate blocking."

"Record her voice. We'll cut to it if we can."

Sophie crossed to Master Control and punched the keycode without looking. Inside smelled like hot plastic and commitment.

"Can we get AM if we lose the chain?"

"Maybe," Marty said, squinting at a CRT he trusted more than God. "If I ride her right and the mast out west loves us."

"It remembers what people sound like. Can't deepfake an um."

Security buzzed. Milan at front desk: *Crowd across street. Not big.*

Shouty. Phones on sticks. Two megaphones. AFP says they'll keep it off the steps.

Sophie typed: *If anyone gets inside, bring them to me. Names before narratives.*

She headed back and wrote a skeleton bulletin in her notebook:

ABC National Bulletin (Draft) Good morning. 04:06. Experiencing outages—power north, banking and comms in parts. Confirmed: Darwin hospitals on generators. Grid prioritizing critical services. Confirmed: Reports of unrest at embassies Jakarta/Manila. Staff safe. Cannot confirm cause. Authorities investigating. Please: Avoid speculation. Prepare for local disruptions. Check neighbors. ABC on AM and FM. Updates :15, :30, :45, top of hour.

The lighting dipped. Came back. Dipped again. Her brain played its disaster playlist: California quakes, Mumbai blackout, Honiara when the generator died.

Her phone: **Aunty Mei**: *You up? Uncle says army choppers. War?*

Not war. Tell Uncle to stop policing the sky.

A Melbourne producer tried crossing to her. The cross-point failed, presenter frozen mid-word.

Sophie lifted her mic. "We go from here. My desk. No graphics."

Marty in her ear: "You're up in ten. Going wide to Sydney. If we fall, you'll still be in kitchens on AM."

"Copy."

Five seconds. She thought of the nurse in Darwin Kailana had mentioned. The port Noah was defending. Cities holding their breath.

Three seconds.

Red tally light.

"Good morning. It's four-oh-six, and if you're watching this, you've noticed the world is sideways."

She spoke like making tea—practical, measured. Confirmed lines first, then the not-yets. She told people where to put their hands. Made the country a kitchen by asking it to check neighbors.

"We'll update at fifteen past the hour." Red light black, back, black.

"Good," Zed whispered.

Outside, Ultimo dawn was false promise. The crowd had grown—signs, phones, chants finding rhythm: *Turn it on, turn it on.*

Milan buzzed: *One wants to talk live. Says 'the truth' in a way that makes me itch.*

Bring him to foyer. No megaphone.

She took the stairs. In the foyer, a bearded young man held a phone-stick, telling it: "The media won't tell you this, but—" He saw her. "—but now they have to."

"Hi. I'm Sophie. If I open this, will you not scream?"

She cracked the door three inches. He leaned in, smelling of keep-cups and certainty.

"They're turning things off," he said. "Banks, news, power. They'll say it's hackers but it's them. Always them. They want a reset—"

"Who's they?"

"We want you to turn it back on. You could if you wanted."

"If we could, we would. Can I put your voice on air? My mic. Two minutes."

He hesitated between being the story and being a source. "Two minutes."

She recorded him talking about cash for petrol like revolution, girlfriend's dead phone, rumors of the bridge shut, trains stopped. He used "they" like scripture.

A bottle broke at the crowd's edge. Glass meeting cement. AFP didn't tense—they'd decided not to at 03:30.

Marty in her ear: "Encoder weirdness. If I lose you, I'll love you in AM."

"Love you back."

A woman with a Woolies bag touched her arm. "My mother's in St George. Dialysis. What do I do?"

"You go. Hospital's ready. If someone says bridge is closed, listen to signs not someone. Keep your radio on."

Milan lifted his chin—inside now. Sophie slipped back.

Unknown number again: *We can help your broadcast. Approve encoder update.*

Send cake, she typed, using Reyes' code.

Soon.

Back at her desk, the software rundown had gone grey with death. Zed had a printout stapled together. "Jakarta audio clean. Darwin—a voice from the port. He sounds like someone who needs a hug."

"Twenty seconds at :15. We're not horror. We're a mirror."

Marty counted her in with hand signals. Red light generous.

"This is ABC. Four-fifteen."

Updates: hospitals, grid, embassies. Dylan's two minutes, temperature right. Check neighbours—repetition as kindness. She said AM like a saint's name.

Halfway through, vision stuttered. Digital burped, swallowed tongue, considered dying. Audio wobbled. Then AM caught—

silver thread in a thousand kitchens, utes with dents, farmhouses where dogs knew that voice.

On the wall, social exploded: thousand posts per minute, same syntax, same misplaced comma. She saw it then—the comma tell. Half the posts had commas where they shouldn't: *Turn it on, tonight* instead of *Turn it on tonight.*

"Botnets," Zed bared teeth. "Same template."

Sophie wrote: **Common template—wrong comma** and circled it like a target.

Marty again in five. Sophie at the mic: "Four-thirty."

Through the first paragraph, second, into third—

Glass at the front made a noise. Not picture anymore. Shouts rolled up like weather. Something hit wet—fruit or paint or slogan. AFP moved, not fast, enough. The crowd convulsed with new voltage. A drone came level with third floor and looked in with its camera grin.

Sophie kept reading. "We will be here."

Red light died. Downstairs glass made second sound. Not crack. Not yet.

"Do we stay?" Zed asked.

"We always stay. That's the job."

Sophie wrote **We stayed** on paper, taped it below the clock. Added: **You did too.**

Outside, Sydney remembered how to be quiet, then forgot, then tried again. The comma tell spreading through posts like a signature. Information warfare meeting real streets.

The hour turned. Darwin burned. Sydney gathered. Between them, a continent holding its breath.

CHAPTER 6: HOUR 05:00
GENERATOR HEARTS

Lieutenant Kailana Reyes

The bunker lights had been trimmed to amber that made everyone look already dead. The main wall showed what they'd kept and what they'd lost: **GRID** with Darwin dark by decision, **CABLE** bitten in three places, **COMMS** mottled, **HOSPITALS** holding, **BASES** steady. The red clock above read 05:00—the hour that pretends morning exists.

Kailana Reyes kept one palm on the console, feeling the grid's pulse through laminate. HVDC held at Stage Three. Twenty minutes of ungainly saves—shaving circuits, feathering trip points, lying to machines about who was in charge. The hospital tile pulsed **GEN** green. The base flickered between **GRID** and **GEN**. The desal plant couldn't decide which parent to trust.

She'd printed two more SITREPs. Dead trees as permanence. They lay flat, edges humming with recycled air.

SITREP 05:00Z+10 HVDC Stage Three armed. Maintaining islanded microgrid. Priority 1: RDH / Priority 2: Desal / Priority 3A: Base SGP-DWN03 three attenuations confirmed, increasing loss at 71km. Darwin Port: internal fire Warehouse C, suspected UUV near shore. Fuel farm strike 03:47—contained, ugly. — Lt. K. Reyes, ADF Defence Comms

Her secure phone vibrated. Monash.

"Reyes."

"Lieutenant." Gravel in a bucket. "Lost our air picture. One stubborn radar and faith. NORFORCE reports wakes off Melville. Border Force shadowed. How's the patient?"

"Stable. Fragile. Hospital on gen, desal fidgeting, base breathing shallow. If HVDC dips again, I cut more of the town."

"Cut what you need. I want the hospital boring."

"Copy." She hesitated. "Sir, the Canberra NAT—"

"We'll burn those logs at dawn. For now, lock the door."

The line clicked. She breathed—four in, four out. Brisbane therapist's freebie that still worked.

On **HOSPITALS**, text appeared: **Fuel reserve 36 hours at current draw. Deliveries uncertain.** She tagged it priority and tapped a note: *Confirm transfer pump redundancy. Manual override?*

A new window bloomed with solicitor's politeness: **Apply stability update? Vendor capsule validated. Urgent.**

Right signature, right everything. She lifted the management uplink clear with two fingers and dropped it in the Faraday pouch next to her pocketknife. The window stayed, now validating against nothing.

"Not today."

The relay yard went amber—temperature rising. She opened thermal overlay. Heat pooling where it shouldn't. She vented louvres. If you anthropomorphized machines, they behaved. Or you behaved.

"Reyes," Corporal Tully from the doorway, young enough shaving was still negotiation. "Base Ops needs eyes on hospital genset. Plant supervisor screaming about transfer hiccup."

"Good instinct not trusting remotes." She grabbed her hardcase—**Edison**, old serial terminal in padded shell with angry labels she'd written. "You're driving."

Outside, Darwin air hit like a wet hand. Smoke from the fuel farms drew a line south. A sound rolled from that direction—not explosion, the groan of something heavy accepting new shape.

"Ma'am," Tully said, "low drone in the lane, you don't hero. Brake and bullbar."

"Yes."

The hospital looked like hospitals do—tired and determined. The generator building sat in concrete, color of old envelopes. Two NT Health engineers, one pale from too much night.

"Reyes?" the pale one, Marnie, said.

"Show me."

Inside, the genset hummed contentment. The control screen listed polite alarms. **TRANSFER PUMP — INTERMITTENT. FREQUENCY — 49.74 Hz** winking like it enjoyed jazz. She laid palm against panel, building the picture.

"We're shedding non-critical. Admin off, cafeteria off. Keeping OR, ICU, NICU, ER, their chillers. Air stays but choked to 19 degrees."

"People will complain."

"The Prime Minister wants babies breathing. She can buy fans later."

Tully at the door, radio up. A curlew screamed. He flinched, then pretended not.

She clipped Edison to the genset's serial port, fed it commands that made modern devices remember their grandparents. The pump alarm had rhythm—on for twenty, off for six. Not random. She pictured a device taped to conduit, not cutting power but suggesting the pump take breaks.

"Check the trunk line," she told Marnie. "Looking for something arrogant with a SIM cage."

They found it under janitorial chemicals. Black tape over brand, pulsing smugly. She pinched the power. Above, **TRANSFER PUMP** went from *INTERMITTENT* to *ACKNOWLEDGED* to quiet.

Her wrist vibrated. She ignored it.

"Fuel?"

"Two tanks. Three if contractor delivers, which he won't."

"We'll pretend. Then scare him."

Her radio hissed. NORFORCE: "Patrol Three. Lights over Shoal Bay. Hum like a fridge. If they were fish, I'd call them patient."

"Eyes only. Don't get curious."

Tully stepped out, scanned, returned. "Ma'am, something low northeast. Not chopper. Two, maybe three."

"Inside. Door."

They shut in with diesel and lemon disinfectant. She watched frequency drift, tapped it back with tiny adjustments. Outside, the base warning siren stretched awake. From the port, another sound—not thunder, wall without bricks.

Secure line lit. Monash.

"Darwin fuel farms report trouble. Port less than it was. Keep hospital breathing, base conscious. Cut everything else."

"CBD goes dark. Traffic lights, malls, coffee. City can be offended later."

"Offend away. And Reyes—good hands."

Twice now. She put the praise aside and got to work. The islanding panel asked bureaucratic questions. She answered with teacher patience and firefighter impatience. Yellow rectangles turned grey as she slid them OFF. The espresso dots went out. She left ABC because someone should believe in radio.

The door rattled soft. Not violent. Gentleman at wrong address. A voice outside, not English, not question. The whine came—drone over the courtyard wall, hovering like indecision.

"Counter-UAS?" Tully asked.

"In a hospital?" Marnie said. "Our counter is 'please don't' and magazines."

"Sprinklers," Kailana said, brain offering stupid miracles. She yanked the emergency valve. Ceiling clunked. Metal groan. Then sprinklers sneezed and the world turned to warm rain.

The drone whine shifted, offended. A black dot drifted into view, not bomb-drone but courier. Magnets and something that liked to eat. It nudged toward the switch cabinet.

Tully fired the extinguisher. The drone bucked in CO_2 cloud, fought, lost, won back. Hit the cabinet with a slap.

"Down," Kailana said, threw herself between switch and unit.

The device sparked. Breaker tripped. Unit shuddered. Marnie swore at pitch that made religion blush and slammed manual bypass. The genset coughed, chose work.

The drone died and slid to wet floor.

Security burst in—two health guards with batons and respect for shins, one NT Police with a night-shift face.

"You okay?"

"Working," Kailana said. There wasn't a box for okay.

Radio hissed. ASD polite Canberra voice: "Darwin, eyes on your management plane again. Parliament NAT lively."

"Negative. We require distance."

"Understood."

Secure line. Monash: "Status?"

"Hospital held. Tick-tack drone met CO_2. City dark, base lit, desal grumpy."

"Good. Canberra arguing about escalation. We're trying not to give them nouns."

"I'll knit them adjectives we don't need."

She swore she heard him almost laugh. "If the air goes loud, stay inside on the wire. You're worth more as hands than a plaque."

A hero with a plaque. Her name on a wall in a hundred years with a QR code and bored students.

"Copy. I like paper, not that much."

Click.

The sprinkler rain thinned. The drone lay like a dead beetle. Marnie smiled at it.

"Thank you," she said to Kailana.

"Later. We'll have cake."

"Soon," Marnie said, and they both blinked at the coincidence.

Text from Ops: **Multiple low-RCS skirting east of city. Counter-UAS to base and farms.** Another: **ABC holding on AM. Bless them.**

Outside, the sky shaded toward morning—disrespectful. She touched the genset's fascia, checking fever. The hum was right.

From the base, a siren switched from steady to waver.

"Inside," she said. "Quiet, we like inside. Loud, we love it."

Another drone crested the fence, arguing with itself, then turned fast toward them.

"Tully."

"I see it."

He waited for distance, then squeezed. White bloom ate drone. It clawed, shivered, lost lift, hit the wall like a dropped plate.

Further off, heavier arrival—fireball from south of port becoming smoke column. The genset didn't flinch.

She looked at the wall clock: 05:59. The next hour leaned against the door.

Darwin breathed. The country wanted to fall. The plant room said later.

CHAPTER 7: HOUR 06:00
ARTICLES OF FAITH

Prime Minister Patricia Keating

By six, the building had learned the crisis gait—fast where necessary, measured everywhere else. The Cabinet ante-room smelled of burnt coffee and controlled panic. On the wall, Australia bled in neat categories: **Darwin dark by design**, **RDH on generators**, **East Arm contained**, **Port operational**. The comma tell Sophie had identified spread across social feeds like a disease with grammar.

"Start," Patricia Keating said.

Vale slid paper across—still warm from printing. "Darwin drone attacks intensified past hour. Hospital genset defended, two drones disabled. Reyes holding the grid by fingernails. East Arm fuel farm—ugly but contained. JORN confidence climbing toward high."

"Casualties?"

"Minor injuries only. Lucky, not sustainable."

Kira pressed her earpiece. "Embassy Jakarta confirms: crowd doubled since midnight. Professional agitators with identical signs—wrong comma in half. Manila degrading. New crowds in Kuala Lumpur, Singapore showing organization."

The room door opened. Reid entered with Foreign Minister

Sarah Park, both immaculate at an hour when nobody should be.

"Prime Minister," Park said, "DFAT recommends immediate Article IV invocation. The Americans—"

"The Americans have one arm broken." Keating kept her voice level. "Their exact words four hours ago."

"That was before coordinated drone strikes on our infrastructure," Park insisted. "This is an act of war."

"This is an act of something. We don't name it until we can prove it."

Reid adjusted his cuff—the tell she'd learned to watch. "Prime Minister, with respect, every hour we delay costs us options. Central coordination would—"

"No remote pushes to critical infrastructure." She turned to Vale. "Has that been absolutely clear?"

"Crystal. Though we've logged seventeen attempts from Parliament NAT in the last two hours."

Keating didn't look at Reid. "Interesting."

Hastings arrived, no longer pretending to have slept. "JORN shows multiple waves forming. Williamtown needs authority for ready-one. East coast will be hit at dawn."

"Move to ready-one. No scramble without violation."

The secure phone rang. She lifted it, knowing who it would be.

"Prime Minister," Monash said, background noise of crisis behind him. "Swarm forming over Arafura. Mix of fixed-wing and rotary. Sophisticated coordination. I'm implementing full defensive posture Darwin and Tindal. Request Williamtown to cockpit-ready."

"Approved. Michael—thresholds?"

"We're walking the edge. No mass casualties yet. No confirmed attribution. But Prime Minister—this is rehearsed. Someone drilled this."

"I know. Hold the line."

She hung up and found the room watching her. Seven hours without sleep had started to show in the margins—hands gripping tables too tight, coffee cups accumulated like evidence.

"Frames," she said. "We are still in frames. Defence—ready-one nationally, full posture north. Home Affairs—activate state emergency centers to standby. Treasury—markets will panic at open. Give them boring words about liquidity. DFAT—"

Her personal phone buzzed. She never checked it during crisis. But the number was her husband's, and he never called during crisis.

"Thirty seconds," she told the room and stepped into the corridor.

"Patricia." His voice carried something she hadn't heard since her mother's diagnosis. "Turn on the news. Any news."

She found a wall monitor, flicked to CNN. The chyron hit like cold water: **MASS CYBER ATTACKS ACROSS US INFRASTRUCTURE. PENTAGON CONFIRMS LIMITED COMMUNICATIONS. NATO ARTICLE 5 CONSIDERATIONS.**

Below, footage of smoke over what looked like Chicago. Another feed showing crowds at the White House gates—same signs, same wrong comma, different language.

She walked back into the room and put her phone down with deliberate calm.

"The United States is under similar attack. NATO considering Article 5. Our situation is not isolated—it's coordinated globally."

Silence detonated.

Reid stood. "Prime Minister, this changes everything. Article IV immediately. Full American support will—"

"Full American support doesn't exist if they can't project power. We invoke Article IV when our conditions are met, not because we're scared."

"You're gambling with the country!"

The room turned. Reid had raised his voice—first time anyone could remember.

Keating met his eyes. "I'm governing it. There's a difference."

Park sided with Reid. "Prime Minister, the public will demand—"

"The public will demand we keep hospitals running and babies breathing. Everything else is commentary."

Vale's phone lit. She read, paled. "Williamtown reports first visual contact. Multiple radar tracks. Swarm density unprecedented."

Keating felt the moment crystallize. Dawn was breaking. The attack they'd defended against piecemeal through the night was about to become something else. She could feel the weight of Article IV in her briefcase, paper that could change a quiet century.

"Cabinet votes," Reid said. Constitutional but aggressive.

"Cabinet advises," Keating corrected. "I decide."

Kira, urgent: "AM broadcast in two minutes. They need a line."

Keating walked to the window. Dawn painted Canberra in false peace. Somewhere, Darwin sweated in humidity and smoke. Sydney crowds grew with manufactured rage. Her mother's voice, years gone: *When the storm comes, be the roof, not the rain.*

She turned back. "We stay at Article III. Conditions for IV remain: mass casualty strike, proven attribution, landing attempt, or restored U.S. capability. Until then, we defend ourselves."

"That's—" Reid started.

"Final." She moved toward the broadcast booth. "Kira, tell Williamtown they have defensive authority. Weapons tight but weapons free on positive hostile."

In the small booth, she faced the microphone that connected her to kitchens and utes and hospital waiting rooms. The red light came on.

"Good morning. This is the Prime Minister. You're seeing dawn, which means we've made it through the night."

She kept her voice steady as steel.

"Our hospitals are running. Our defence forces are protecting critical infrastructure. Some of you lost power—you helped each other through intersections and shared torches with strangers. That's who we are."

She could feel Reid listening, waiting for her to say war.

"We're consulting with allies. We're defending our shores. We are not panicking, and we are not pretending this is normal. We are working. Stay with your radios. Check on neighbors. We'll speak again in an hour."

Red light off. She walked back to find the room exactly as she'd left it—except Reid was on his phone, turned away, speaking quietly.

"Marcus," she said.

He ended the call. "Updating my office."

"Your office that's been trying to push updates through Parliament NAT all night?"

His smile didn't reach his eyes. "Technical staff trying to help."

"Technical staff need to keep their hands to themselves."

The secure line rang. She knew before answering—the weight of what was coming pressed through the air itself.

"Prime Minister," Monash said. "First wave inbound. Time to light them up."

Through the window, the sun broke the horizon. Beautiful and indifferent.

Day Zero had become Day One.

CHAPTER 8: HOUR 07:00
SWARM

Major General Michael Monash

The morning over Darwin had the color of old steel. Humid air pressed down. From the ops floor, the harbour looked like glass nobody wanted to touch.

"Local scope still intermittent," Hargreaves said, hunched over his console. "JORN pushing MED to HIGH on low-RCS trending south."

Julia Ng slid fresh paper under Monash's hand—still warm. **City dark by order, hospital gen holding, base lit, desal uneasy**. In the margin, Reyes's handwriting: *Cooling corridors mapped. Can over-provision pumps for foam. No remote pushes.*

He looked at the wall. **GRID**: Darwin a deliberate grey smear. **HOSPITALS**: green with one amber line—**FUEL 36 HRS @ DRAW. BASES**: steady. **COMMS**: bruised but working. **PORT**: strip of cameras, one blind, one blinking.

"NORFORCE, Cobourg," a coastal voice came in. "Lights running low. Like they owe someone money. Hum like a fridge. Parallel to shore."

"Keep distance. Report, don't intercept."

On the PORT feed, East Arm's white tanks sat behind earthen bunds, manifold racks glinting. A forklift abandoned at diagonal. Single gull.

The hum arrived in his teeth first—crown vibration. High and even, dying fluorescent.

"Sounders at East Arm picking up smalls, multiple, low-fast, mixed altitude."

Hargreaves's radar coughed up dots. Not weather. Chess pieces being arranged.

"Vector?"

"Two prongs. One toward runway infrastructure. One straight for fuel depot."

Monash leaned in. The room leaned with him.

"All stations, Swarm Response One. Army C-UAS teams to East Arm—EW jammers B/E bands, airburst 40mm overwatch, no uncontrolled fire over tanks. Firecomms, all units to depot perimeter. Foam monitors manual. Cooling corridors along bunds and manifolds. AFP—shut the road. Border Force—eyes only."

"Copy," came the chorus.

"Get me depot superintendent."

A voice like cigarettes and hoses: "Havel, depot."

"You're about to have guests. Counter-UAS and fire on apron in two. Don't cluster. Buddy pairs. Scrub anything that looks like a Christmas present taped wrong."

"I like boring presents."

The air shimmered, then broke into detail. Fixed-wing microdrones skimmed water like swallows, popped the bank. Second layer higher: fat quadcopters with payload ports, YouTube lessons learned. The third layer he couldn't see yet but felt between his eyes.

"EW up," Army sergeant called. "DroneShield live. Painting

B/E bands."

Quadcopters twitched and fell into gravel. Others didn't care—jerked, found inertial, pressed on.

"Pre-programmed," Hargreaves said. "Jam the leash, they run the route."

First hits at fence line and pump-house. Pops, precise, shaped charges cutting steel. Spark showers. A ute near Gate Three jumped, settled, horn keening.

"East Arm, Forty-Six at bund Bravo. Foam monitor engaged. Cooling line established."

"Keep people under cover."

Quadcopters dived at the manifold. One stuck. One bounced, magnet seeking panel. Flash. Arc. Flame finding welcome and growing.

"Ignition on manifold. Station Two, advance your line!"

A firefighter in yellow stepped into frame, became smaller than the thing before him. Foam went white and righteous. Flame considered, chose to continue. Heat bloomed orange to white, too fast.

"C-UAS engaging fixed-wings. Forty mil airburst."

Launchers thumped. Flares stitched air. Two deltas tumbled smoking. Three more crossed and kissed Tank 12's dome with magnets.

"They're aiming for vent stacks," Ng said, losing neutrality. "We lose those, pressure cook."

"Foam the domes. Cool everything."

A quad hit the gate camera. Picture black. Another camera showed gate as white smear—fire sunlight. Air went feral on every mic.

"Reyes, can you give Firecomms extra draw? Accept

brownouts anywhere except NICU and base."

"Already shoving pumps forward," she said, calm from her fluorescent room. "Desal dip in ten."

"Good hands."

An Army private fired a DroneGun like a tuba at a wasp. Drone twitched, accepted gravity. He whooped. Second drone arrived indignant, slapped charge into the ute behind him. Windshield gone. His corporal dragged him behind concrete, teaching humility in eight words.

"Havel, blowdown plan?"

"The one where we don't poison the harbour? Saint and miracle. We can vent to sacrificial pit. It's ugly."

"Get people off catwalks. Bund Bravo priority. If Tank 12's vents go, we accept a pit."

"There's a kid on Tank 12."

Camera swung. Figure in yellow on dome's ladder, cutting something that didn't belong.

"Call her down. Now."

"She's stubborn. She does the job that keeps other jobs possible."

"Tell her I said later."

Fixed-wings adjusted—climbed twenty meters, new approach. Airburst bloomed. Three disintegrated. Five slipped through.

"Flashback through line three!" Firecomms voice swallowed. "Shutting three. Four holding."

A quadcopter rode foam's edge, reached under pipe with its payload. Kissed steel. Pipe sighed, seam gave, flame said hello.

"Need more forty-mil. Can't use rifles without making YouTube tutorials on detonating fuel farms."

"Make your shots count."

On the wall, **COMMS** blinked: **ABC AM HOLDING**. Thin thread of steadiness. Woman's voice telling kitchens to fill kettles, old mast doing math with vacuum tubes. The thought sat for half a breath.

Hargreaves twisted dials. "Sir, there's another layer."

"I know."

Third wave announced with zipper sound. Microjets—larger, too fast for comfort. Low over mangroves, popped up, threw darts. Submunitions with brains he couldn't afford.

"Everyone under cover. This isn't schoolyard."

Darts stitched bund wall. One found weakness, talked about it. Wall held. Conversation continued. Concrete the size of a mattress decided it didn't belong.

"Commence blowdown to sacrificial," Havel hoarse. "Pit's lined but the frogs will write letters."

"Do it. EPA on pre-brief. We owe them a conference and a hug."

The kid from the ladder appeared at ground, soaked, furious, alive. Havel swore at her for form, then put hand on shoulder because humans are real.

"New bands. They're frequency-agile. We hop, they hop."

"Lead. Make them follow."

Tank 12 pumped darkness into guilt-colored pit. Bund steamed. Foam crawled across gravel. Fire roared with everything it wanted.

"Cape Byron reports shadow resumed. Whatever's out there doesn't want fame."

"They launched from something pretending to be fishing," Hargreaves murmured. "They'll be cross if we call them navy."

"Adjectives later. Verbs now."

A quad descended with dentist patience, nudged cabinet. Private stepped out, swung shotgun, checked himself, fired tight pattern. Quad became lesson.

"Two civilian utes attempting entry to 'help'. AFP intercepting."

"Turn them around gently."

Hargreaves's screen stuttered. "Gap between waves. Thirty seconds to breathe."

"Breathe. Reposition, reload, rethink. Firecomms—push foam where heat says you'll wish."

On camera, firefighter who'd been too small crouched behind ladder drinking while buddy patted shoulder: alive/alive/alive. The kid in yellow rolled cable like rewinding film.

"Prime Minister on secure," Ng said.

"Patricia," Monash said, setting civility aside. "Engaged at East Arm. Layered swarms. Jammers effective on leashed, less on pre-programmed. Hits at manifold and dome vents. One tank to sacrificial. Foam holding. No civilian fatalities yet."

"Authority stands. Use what you need. I'll wear the frogs and headlines. Williamtown ready-one. Do you need east assets?"

"Negative. This is local. Save east for when horizon moves."

"Good hands."

Quadcopters regrouped silently. Microjets lined up like men showing off. Sergeant's hand dropped. Airburst stitched. Three jets coughed sideways into salt. Two reached bund, wrote regret on concrete. Foam hissed psalms.

Third wave slackened. Not gone. Thinking.

Hargreaves peeped. "Fewer toys. Running out or saving for next party."

"Or they've done what they came for," Ng said.

Manifold camera settled. Foam deep enough to swallow boots. Single late drone bumped cabinet, fell over drunk.

"Head on it," Firecomms said. "Bunds hot but intact. Twelve cooling. Blowdown pit's a sin for later. Black on line three, can live without. One minor, one wrist. Everyone recognizable to mothers."

"Hold perimeter. Don't call it. This quiet thinks it's clever."

On the wall, Jakarta fattened, Manila flickered, Sydney CBD darker than it liked. Inland AM transmitter hanging on.

"Status boards. Three lines."

Ng rattled: "East Arm contained and ugly. Base lit and breathing. City dark by design. Hospital steady. Desal sulky."

He stepped back, let the room's hum pass through him. Thought of Reyes with hand on panel, kid in yellow rolling cable, private learning humility. His mother's kitchen radio making mornings logical.

"Reset ammunition. Rotate crews. Hydrate. This isn't the last hour."

Smoke laid dark sentence across harbour pointing at horizon. Bund steamed. Foam glowed. A gull screamed at the world.

Hargreaves's scope swept clean, returned empty sky.

"Sir, for the moment—"

"Don't name it."

He looked at the clock: 07:59.

"Tell Reyes keep city dark. Tell Havel frogs get my apology. Tell Firecomms they get hero sandwiches when this is past tense."

"And you?" Ng asked.

He picked up the handset. "I call the Prime Minister and tell her this hour didn't break us."

The second hand clicked. The depot had held. The swarm had been bloodied but not destroyed. Somewhere offshore, something that wanted to be innocent was thinking about the next delivery.

War had properly begun.

CHAPTER 9: HOUR 08:00
CLEAN SKY

Flight Lieutenant Sienna Crossman

The scramble horn cut through Williamtown's morning.

Sienna Crossman was already moving—helmet under arm, legs eating tarmac. The crew chief jogged beside her. The sky over the base was clean blue that lied about everything. Beyond the dunes, the Pacific held its counsel.

"Viper One," the liney yelled over turbine whine. "You're hot. Two-ship. Overwatch has vectors."

"Copy." She climbed the ladder. The cockpit wrapped itself around her—familiar angles teaching hands where to live. Helmet on, visor down, world narrowed to symbols and light. Her breathing settled. Adrenaline made the run; ritual made the cockpit home.

The Pratt spooled with a cough becoming statement. Vibration through the seat: *I'm awake.*

"Viper One, taxi," Ground called.

"Viper One rolling." To her wingman: "Two, check."

"Two," Nikki Parnell's voice—clean with the thin smile that meant business.

Canopy sealed. World became film with sound down. Crew in

orange moved their old dance. A magpie on a fencepost watched the fighter roll past—another Tuesday in its world.

"Overwatch confirms arming complete."

"Fox-two plus gun." Two AIM-9X, 25mm ready. No AMRAAM—the planners had decided this morning was knife-fight range.

"Picture: multiple low-RCS tracks inbound coastal from northeast. Angels low to five. Speed variable, swarm behavior. Primary axis Newcastle-Kooragang. Secondary scattered along coast. Rules are scramble-on-violation. Intercept on hostile act. Threat origin unknown."

Unknown. The word everyone was too professional to replace with what they suspected.

"Tower, Viper Flight ready."

"Cleared immediate, winds zero-eight-zero at ten."

She pushed. The jet ran. Nose light, weight off, gear up. Coast sliding left. Tomaree Head passing. Heading zero-niner-zero, low, the sound cutting morning.

The helmet fed her the fusion. EOTS finding warm insects along water. APG-81 painting arcs of things trying to be small. DAS showing dots and lines. The jet making it all into language.

"Overwatch, Viper has tally on group one. Multiple smalls, split at two hundred AGL, thirty seconds to coast. Confirm rules if they cross infrastructure."

"Confirmed. Make them stop."

First drones slipped past Stockton—fixed-wing deltas, fast and polite. Above them, quadcopters with bellies full of intentions. If they took the rail bridge, Kooragang's spine would break. If they touched the tanks, the morning would turn.

"Two, bracket. I'll push the fat ones. You cut deltas."

"Two." Nikki eased off with relish.

Sienna came right, nose down. World flattened to intent. She cued the lead quad. The 9X pipped happiness. Thumb. Missile left like a cat with purpose. Found quad, removed its argument. She dropped nose for gun.

GAU-22 spat its line. Rounds traced lace. One drone folded embarrassed. Another tried pretending, then admitted. The rest scattered.

"Overwatch, splash two. Gunning."

"Two, splash three. Bridge breathing."

"Keep tanks alive. East Arm sends regards."

She rolled into the fight. The tanks below—shapes from cadet days—now had names and faces. Foam gunners were dots in yellow she'd never meet but loved anyway.

A quad tried for the manifold. She stitched it. Another learned about consequences.

Something bigger on periphery—long-body UAV, ten meters, running waves like a ruler. She tagged it. The 9X offered joy. She put it where the long-body would be after its lie. Missile wrote *no*. Long-body lost argument with sea.

"Any higher reads on origin?"

"AIS is poetry. One track's a fishing boat that acts like a seminar. Another doesn't exist but keeps being somewhere."

The jet murmured fuel. She checked numbers. Plenty for this. Not for generosity.

"Ground," Overwatch said softer, "Darwin sends gratitude. Lieutenant Reyes appreciates your form."

Flat voice: "Tell Darwin we'll keep their east from catching."

A thread slid across display—*Darwin Comms: pump priority maintaining—hospital/base steady.* Some sysadmin had found a path for one consolation. She filed it where she kept her reasons.

"Two, your right. Cluster at seventy, taking sand like they own it."

She rolled low enough to smell beach. Gun rumbled. Sand spat offended. Three quads discovered Newton.

A helpline tone: "Sydney reports drone over Harris Street—media site. AFP asks we avoid downtown kinetic. Ground has it. Your zone Newcastle. Kooragang priority."

"Copy." Somewhere in Darwin, a woman with braided hair was telling machines to behave. It made the cockpit less alone.

More mosquitoes along the canal. She went vertical, rolled, put half-second of gun in center. They scattered. One fought back into line. One round where its sentence wanted finishing.

"Overwatch, picture south?"

"Two and Three pushing to Pittwater. Counter-UAS along grid with gaps. Rail substation needs to breathe, hospital wants to keep breathing. You're keeping Kooragang boring."

A quad tried the vent. She taught it consequences.

Her gut tagged a dotted line at sea—movements like small truths becoming bigger lie. AIS said **FISH**. Her gut said liar. Filed for later.

"Fuel check."

"Two good. One hero heading for rail."

She came left. Slow quad with big idea. Gentle tap. Four pieces.

"Newcastle calming. Kooragang crews report holding. East Arm thumbs-up. Spurts south, but other flights on them. New vector over water later—origin unclear. Clear to hold then recover."

"You don't want me fishing?" Nikki disappointed.

"Save appetite."

Sienna climbed to humane altitude. City below, stubborn. Tank domes silver. Foam like lace. Yellow dots thinking and sweating and making the next hour possible. The tiny specific love for place—not flags but nurses and radios.

"Two, form. Courtesy lap then home before the jet complains."

They came along the Hunter. Kooragang left, Stockton right. Pelican rose from sandbar, kept opinion private. She waggled once at foam crews—ridiculous but human.

"Viper Flight, recover."

She touched down light—cup on saucer. The jet rolled satisfied. Crew chief climbed with a grin trying not to be. She popped canopy. Day rushed in, hot and civilian.

"Looked like swatting mozzies, ma'am."

"Big ones," Nikki said from next bay. "With chemistry degrees."

Sienna unlatched, handed jet back with a pat that would embarrass her if named.

In Darwin, two thousand kilometers away, the fused picture steadied for seconds. A secondary screen showed **VIPER-1**, neat arc over Kooragang with small flares where problems stopped.

Lieutenant Kailana Reyes, hand on panel, eyes on too much, allowed herself another pair for this second.

She saw the arc. The tidy dots. The way returns moved like someone who trusted their hands.

"God," she said, unprofessional and true. "She's good."

HVDC hummed under palm. Hospital stayed green. Base held. Out over Williamtown, Sienna Crossman taxied in, and across rooms and heads and wires, two women who'd never met kept each other's mornings from becoming worse.

The skirmishes were spreading. Nobody had said invasion. Nobody had declared anything. But the pattern was there for those willing to see—tested defences, probed responses, measured capabilities.

The Pacific was choosing sides without naming them.

CHAPTER 10: HOUR 09:00
UNILATERAL ORDERS

Major General Michael Monash

The ops floor smelled of foam residue and exhaustion. Smoke from East Arm still wrote its accusation across the harbour. On the wall, **GRID** showed Darwin dark by choice, **HOSPITALS** green but hungry, **BASES** steady, **PORT** contained. The **COMMS** pane blinked like a dying eye.

The ops floor smelled of foam residue and exhaustion. Smoke from East Arm still wrote its accusation across the harbour. On the wall, **GRID** showed Darwin dark by choice, **HOSPITALS** green but hungry, **BASES** steady, **PORT** contained. The **COMMS** pane blinked like a dying eye.

"Secure Canberra is down," Julia Ng said, voice carrying the weight of what that meant. "PMO line fails. NCM bridge fails. DFAT, ASD—intermittent. We've got NT Government on copper like it's 1986."

Monash let the news sit. Then pushed his chair back and stood. Early forties, carrying scars from the Darwin Protocols, about to make another decision that would define his command.

"Record," he said.

Ng nodded. A corporal hit REC. The red light came on—their judge.

"Time 0900 local. Chief of Joint Operations North, acting as commander JTF NORTH, under delegated authority and in absence of Commonwealth direction due to communications outage. I am elevating Darwin defence posture to FULL."

Not the American words. Not "DEFCON." Just numbers and geography and the weight of deciding alone.

"Orders as follows. One: Base Defence Plan KESTREL to ALERT RED—Darwin and Tindal implement hardened posture, disperse aircraft, restrict surface movement. Two: LAND 19 batteries ring East Arm, Hospital, Darwin base—NASAMS up, RBS-70 forward, weapons tight, hostile by default inside fence. Three: C-UAS maintain jamming, expand bands, no uncontrolled fire over tanks or hospital. Four: NORFORCE to coastal interdiction Cobourg to Tiwi—report, don't engage unless fired upon."

The room breathed once. He continued.

"Five: Harbour Master—civilian movements suspended. AIS off for local shipping. Six: AFP perimeter hard at ABC, RDH, water treatment. Seven: Darwin stays islanded. Hospital and base priority. Eight: Firecomms—foam corridors remain."

He looked at Ng. "Witnessed?"

"Witnessed." Her pen moved with the precision of someone refusing to let crisis take her handwriting.

"Hargreaves, local scope?"

"Prettiest since three a.m.—which means not pretty. Small returns offshore. Gap between waves holding."

"EW—start deception beacons. Give them ghosts and dead alleys."

"Copy. We'll build them a dance floor."

The copper phone rang. Harbour Master, voice like gravel in oil: "Two private utes trying to launch jet-skis 'to help.'

Internet's made everyone a hero."

"Turn them around. Kindly first."

On COMMS, the PMO icon went green to amber to grey. DFAT blinked and sulked. ASD showed a frozen face, then nothing.

"Parliament NAT?" Monash asked, knowing.

"Still poking. Reyes has Darwin keys. We're not touching anything from here."

"We're a country, not a company."

"Sir," Hargreaves said soft. "NORFORCE reports odd sound offshore. Like a fridge and whisper."

"Eyes only."

The secure handset—dead weight. He set it down gently.

"Julia, draft Record of Decision. 'FULL posture—JTF NORTH—absence of direction—immediacy of threat—measures proportionate—civilian protection primary—minimal force.' Stamp it. PM's signature when the world remembers phones."

"Already on paper."

He lifted the open channel. "Havel."

"Bund holds. Pit uglier than divorce. Frogs will sue in slime. But breathing."

"Stagger your refuellers. No heroes."

NT Government on copper. The Premier's sandpaper voice: "Monash, SES wants showgrounds for folks you blacked out. Yes?"

"Yes. Feed them. Water them. No panic."

"Good on you."

A thread blinked from Woomera—latency he could taste:

Southern orbits preserved. Secure path possible on request. Ng saw it. He nodded once. Later.

"Sir," C-UAS major, "RBS-70 teams positioned. NASAMS establishing. Ugly but useful in five."

"ASD shadow relay via WA. We'll pocket it," Ng murmured.

He opened Darwin channel. "Reyes."

"Still here."

"City stays dark. Base and hospital greedy. If you need to drop airport precinct—"

"I will. And someone keeps asking for 'stability update.' I keep offering cake."

He almost smiled. "We accept cake. We decline malware."

Hargreaves: "New cluster northeast. Stragglers or testers."

"Hold fire unless inside fence or hostile. No freelancing."

A tech ran up with a map—pen circles around substations, water valves, hospital feeds. "From Reyes. She's drawn arteries."

"AFP to babysit. No lights."

Defence Space Command joined—colonel backlit by antennas. "Elevated noise on LEO links. Priority blackout protocols to preserve space-domain if terrestrial fails."

"Hold at colonel level."

The Army major lifted a hand. "NT Police request lights-out discipline beyond CBD. They want to starve the next wave of visual fixes."

"Granted. Anyone who complains can write sonnets later."

"Captain O'Kearney at Tindal requests dispersal to contingency strip. 'Two baskets' rule."

"Approved."

On the wall, ABC ticker: *AM stable. PM statement held. Public calm, mostly.*

"Everyone drinks water. Eats rectangles that lie about food. We're not heroes. We're plumbers."

Small laugh. Relief finding a chair.

"To the record: JTF NORTH full posture due to comms loss with Canberra. Measures proportionate to continuing events. Civilian life primary. Attribution unassigned."

The red dot watched. He turned to it. "We neither guess nor are goaded."

Hargreaves: "Gap widens. They're deciding whether to come back angry or pretend they never came."

"Let's give them reasons to pretend."

Ng slid the Record under his hand. He signed with neat block letters. She counter-signed. The corporal stamped. Small gavel sound.

"Transmit to NT Government. Hand-carry to base commanders."

Woomera pulsed: *Southern window remains. Use on signal.*

"Not yet. Last tricks for last."

Young comms tech, freckled: "RDH complains about aircon in admin. Twenty-eight degrees."

"File under alive."

The ops floor exhaled. Discipline, not relief.

The secure handset stayed dead. He put his palm on the table, felt the building's pulse.

"Julia, call me the minute you get the PM, even if mid-sentence. Until then, this is our weather."

"Aye."

He looked at PORT—foam lazy, steam lifting. HOSPITALS—green. BASES—steady. COMMS—bruised. WORLD—crowds doing what crowds do. The coin in his pocket untouched.

The weight of the decision sat clean. He'd elevated to full military posture without civilian authority. In peacetime, court martial. In whatever this was—necessity.

His father would have called it "earning your pay the hard way." The PM would either back him or burn him when communications returned. But Darwin would be ready for whatever came next.

"Back to work," he said.

The room obeyed the only order that mattered.

CHAPTER 11: HOUR 10:00
THE MOLE

Prime Minister Patricia Keating

The Cabinet Room felt smaller when the screens wouldn't behave. Two ministers in person, four by video that kept freezing, three by voice on a bridge that came and went like conscience. The air conditioning had been set to bureaucratic neutral—the temperature at which nobody was comfortable enough to fall asleep.

On the wall, Australia showed its wounds: **Darwin dark by design, RDH green on generators, East Arm contained, Newcastle defended**. The **COMMS** pane was mottled—satcom hanging on, microwave gasping, fiber dead in three places. **WORLD** had new circles: **Berlin, Chicago, Mumbai.** Each with the same wrong comma in their protests.

"Let's get the noise on the table," Keating said, taking the head without ceremony. "Defence first."

Hastings leaned forward, sleeves rolled, tie like a noose he'd given up fighting. "We're past probing. East Arm was sophisticated—layered, coordinated with cyber. Williamtown kept Newcastle breathing but we can't be everywhere. Darwin's presumably implementing contingencies but we've lost secure comms. If we keep waiting to name this—"

"We name what we can prove," Keating said. "ASD?"

The Deputy Director's face filled the screen, collar open, papers forgotten in one hand. "Spoofed capsules continuing. Pre-positioned implants across multiple vendors. The attack chains have Chinese-language build artefacts, Russian obfuscation, Iranian TTPs. Either it's coalition or someone wants us thinking coalition."

"Or someone wants us arguing about it while infrastructure burns," Reid said from the corner, having arrived late but perfectly dressed.

Home Affairs on audio, grandmother's patience: "States at emergency centers half-power. AFP holding at media sites. Hospitals outside Darwin stable. But Prime Minister—we're seeing organization. The comma tell Sophie Kerr identified? It's in twelve languages now. Same error, same timing."

"DFAT?"

The Foreign Secretary adjusted his glasses. "Jakarta embassy surrounded but safe. Manila deteriorating. Tokyo asking what's happening. Seoul nervous. Wellington offering quiet help." He paused. "Washington is... complicated."

The room tightened.

"Define complicated."

"State reachable on one line with forty-second latency. DoD split—Hawaii has eyes, continental US conferencing when they can. Their exact words: 'Don't activate anything you can't sustain without us for seventy-two hours.'"

Reid stood, smooth as oil. "Prime Minister, this is exactly why we need Article IV now. The pattern is clear—global coordination, infrastructure targeting, civil disruption. Every hour we delay—"

"Every hour we delay, we keep our options," Keating said. "Article IV means we're declaring this an armed attack requiring military response. Once that genie's out—"

"The genie's already out!" Reid's voice cracked higher than she'd ever heard. "Darwin's burning, Sydney's next, and you're debating grammar!"

Treasury raised a tentative hand on screen. "Markets open in fifty minutes. Without clear position, we'll see panic selling."

"Then give them boring words about liquidity and contingency," Keating said.

Reid pulled out his phone, typing rapidly. "I'm updating my department—"

"You're updating nobody." Keating's voice could have frozen water. "Put it down."

He looked up, and for the first time she saw something underneath the polish. Not concern. Calculation.

"Prime Minister, respectfully, my department needs—"

"Your department needs to stop trying to push updates through Parliament NAT. Seventeen attempts last night, Marcus. Want to explain?"

The room went still.

Reid's smile didn't reach his eyes. "Technical staff trying to help."

"Technical staff trying to access repeater configurations at midnight."

"To stabilise the network—"

"To compromise it."

Hastings's hand had moved to the table's edge, knuckles white. "You're suggesting—"

"I'm stating facts," Keating said. "Someone with Reid's office credentials has been trying to access critical infrastructure all night. Same time as the attacks."

Reid's face didn't change, but something shifted—like watching ice form under water. "That's a serious accusation."

"It's a serious night."

Vale slid a paper across—printout of NAT logs. Timestamps. Reid's office. Over and over.

"Coincidence," Reid said.

"Seventeen coincidences?"

The secure phone rang. Everyone jumped. Keating grabbed it.

"Prime Minister?" Not Monash. ASD Director himself, calling from somewhere that echoed. "We've detained two foreign nationals at a Marrickville warehouse. Printing equipment, RF devices, and computers with the attack templates. The comma tell was deliberate—a signature to track reach."

"Attribution?"

"Working on it. But Prime Minister—they had parliamentary passes. Visitor passes sponsored by—"

Keating looked at Reid. "Let me guess."

"Deputy NSA office," the Director confirmed.

Reid stood slowly, straightening his jacket. "I can explain—"

"Sit down, Marcus."

He didn't sit. "You don't understand the full picture. Central coordination would have prevented—"

"AFP are on their way up," Keating said. "You can explain to them."

His hand went to his pocket. Not for a phone. Hastings was already moving, old soldier reflexes. Reid's hand came out empty but his face had changed completely—the polish gone, replaced by something older and angrier.

"You think this is about politics?" Reid said. "This is about evolution. The old order is done. Australia can either be part of the new architecture or be consumed by it."

"And you decided for us?"

"I decided to survive." His smile returned, cold. "The attacks will continue whether you arrest me or not. The pattern is global. Inevitable. You can either manage the transition or—"

The door opened. AFP officers, quiet and professional.

Reid looked at Keating once more. "Article IV won't save you. The Americans can't project. The region is reorganizing. You're playing yesterday's game."

They led him out. The room sat stunned.

"Jesus," Hastings breathed.

Keating felt the weight of it—not just betrayal but the implication. If Reid had been inside, who else? How deep? How long?

Kira leaned in. "Prime Minister, we've lost Darwin comms completely. Monash is presumably implementing contingencies but—"

"But we don't know what he's deciding," Keating finished.

Vale looked at the wall. Berlin's circle had grown. Chicago showed smoke. Mumbai had gone dark. The pattern Reid mentioned—visible now to anyone willing to see.

"It's not random," Treasury said quietly. "It's coordinated global destabilization."

"Without declaring war," DFAT added. "Because modern war doesn't declare itself."

Keating stood, walked to the window. Canberra looked peaceful. Deceptive. Somewhere Darwin was making decisions without her. Sydney was about to wake up angry. And Reid—Reid had just confirmed what she'd suspected but hoped was paranoia.

This wasn't an attack on Australia. Australia was just one front in something bigger.

"We stay at Article III," she said, turning back. "Conditions for IV remain unchanged: mass casualties, proven state attribution, landing attempt, or restored US capability."

"Patricia—" Hastings started.

"We don't escalate into a conflict we can't define against an enemy we can't name with allies who can't respond."

Her phone buzzed. Husband: *Reid on news being arrested. What's happening?*

She texted back: *The world is reorganizing itself. We're trying to keep our piece.*

"Next moves," she said. "DFAT—back channel to Beijing and Moscow. Don't accuse. Just ask if they're seeing similar patterns. Treasury—boring words to markets. Home Affairs—double AFP at all critical infrastructure."

"And Darwin?" Hastings asked.

"Darwin does what it needs to. Monash has my pre-authorization. When comms restore, we'll either congratulate or court-martial him."

Vale's phone lit. She read, paled. "Woomera reports they can establish emergency command channel via southern window. Audio only. Heavily degraded. But possible."

Keating thought about it. Contact with Darwin versus revealing capability.

"Not yet," she decided. "We keep that card until we need it."

The clock showed 10:47. Reid's empty chair sat like an accusation. Outside, a maintenance crew worked on the lawn, oblivious to the continent reorganizing itself around them.

The world wasn't declaring war. It was just choosing new management. Without asking.

CHAPTER 12: HOUR 11:00
EVIDENCE CHAIN

Noah Tan

The evacuation convoy dumped them at a police checkpoint where Tiger Brennan met desperation. The sun had climbed to that Darwin angle that made everything look overexposed and underdone. Noah's ring binder had gained weight with every page of evidence—thermal prints, timestamps, photos of devices that shouldn't exist.

"You're with me," the AFP officer said—the one with sand in her hair who'd driven him out. "We're checking substations. Looking for more presents from your fresh-vest friends."

They rolled through streets that couldn't decide if they were evacuating or spectating. Some shops had opened out of stubbornness. Others had boards up like they'd seen this movie before. At every intersection, people negotiated the dead traffic lights with a courtesy that would have made anarchists weep.

Radio news crackled: "...Deputy National Security Advisor Marcus Reid arrested... parliamentary passes linked to foreign nationals... Prime Minister maintains Article Three stance..."

"Reid," Noah said. "He was pushing the updates."

"The ones you kept refusing with cake jokes?"

"Reyes taught me that. When someone offers help at midnight, offer them cake instead."

The officer almost smiled. "We're about to need a bakery."

They pulled up at Substation 7 near the Winnellie depot. A crowd had gathered—maybe forty people, signs already printed. **TURN IT ON TONIGHT**. Half with the comma wrong: **TURN IT ON, TONIGHT**. Same font. Same handles that looked bought in bulk.

"There," Noah pointed. Three men in fresh hi-vis at the crowd's edge, not chanting, just watching. One had a backpack with corners that suggested boxes. Another kept touching his ear like he was listening to something.

"Stay in the vehicle," the officer said.

"I need to check the cabinet."

"After we thin this out."

She stepped out, hand on radio. Two more AFP units had appeared, casual but present. Then, from a council truck that had seen better decades, music erupted. **Flame Trees** at a volume that made windows opinions.

The crowd stuttered. Half started singing without meaning to. The fresh-vest men looked at each other with the expression of people whose script had been edited without permission.

Noah slipped out while everyone was distracted, moved along the fence line to the cabinet. Green metal box, utility bland, the kind of infrastructure that became invisible until it stopped working.

He ran his hand under the lip. Nothing. Checked the vents. Clean. Then he saw it—fresh scratches on the lock housing. Someone had been here but interrupted.

A hand on his shoulder. He flinched, turned. Not fresh-vest—a kid, maybe nineteen, holding a phone like a weapon.

"You're one of them," the kid said. "The ones keeping it off."

"I'm the one keeping hospitals running," Noah said. "There's a difference."

"They said you could turn it on if you wanted."

"They lied. It's not a switch. It's thousands of decisions that have to happen in order." He showed the kid his binder. "See this? Evidence of people trying to break those decisions. Make them happen wrong."

The kid looked uncertain. Behind him, the crowd had fully fractured into singers and chanters. The fresh-vest men were retreating, professional rather than panicked.

Noah's phone buzzed. Reyes: *Reid arrested. Parliament NAT was his. Keep documenting.*

He photographed the lock scratches, the crowd, the signs with their deliberate error. In his binder, he wrote: **Winnellie Substation 7—attempted entry, interrupted. Crowd with templates. Music disruption effective.**

The officer returned. "Clean?"

"They tried but didn't finish."

"Pattern's changing. They're getting interrupted more." She looked at the crowd, now mostly just confused people holding signs they weren't sure about. "Someone leaked Reid's arrest. The organized ones are pulling back."

They hit three more substations. Each had the same story—scratches on locks, crowds that dissolved when music played, fresh-vest observers who melted away when noticed. At Palmerston, they found something different.

The cabinet was open.

Inside, a device that hadn't been there yesterday—black box, professional, with cables spliced into the main bus. Not the crude magnetic cans from earlier. This was infrastructure-grade. Permanent.

"Don't touch it," the officer said. "EOD first."

Noah photographed everything. Serial numbers. Cable gauges. The splice pattern that looked like someone had learned it from a manual written in another language but translated carefully. He drew the configuration in his binder, noting: **Evolution from cans to permanent installation. They're embedding.**

His phone lit up with a message from a number he didn't recognize: *Storage unit 19, Berrimah Industrial. One hour. Come alone.*

He showed the officer.

"That's bait," she said.

"Or it's someone with conscience."

She looked at him—properly looked. "You're civilian. You don't have to—"

"My sister's in Singapore. If this spreads there—" He stopped. "I'm already in it."

She called it in. Five minutes later: "We'll ghost you. Three units, no lights. You go in, we watch. First sign of trouble, we flood it."

The storage facility sat in industrial nowhere, the kind of place that existed because sometimes you needed to put things where nobody would care. Unit 19's roller door was up six inches. Enough to suggest. Not enough to see.

Noah lifted it. Inside, lit by a single fluorescent that wanted retirement, was a workspace. 3D printers. Laser cutter. Resin vats. And on the central table, boxes of the magnetic cans, sorted by size.

But the real prize was the wall—covered in maps. Darwin. Sydney. Brisbane. Each with substations marked, some circled in red (complete), others in yellow (attempted), others in green (planned). Times written beside each. A coordination masterpiece.

He photographed everything, hands shaking slightly. In his binder: **Complete attack template discovered. Multiple cities. Timed coordination.**

A sound behind him. He turned. A woman stood in the doorway—mid-forties, exhausted, wearing a Telstra contractor shirt that had seen actual work.

"You're Noah Tan," she said. Not a question.

"Who are you?"

"Someone who thought they were upgrading infrastructure." She held out a thumb drive. "Everything's on here. Work orders. Payment trails. The moment I realized the updates weren't updates."

"Why?"

"Because I have kids. Because Reid came to my office three months ago talking about efficiency and resilience and I believed him." Her voice cracked. "Because I helped build the backdoors and I need someone to know so they can close them."

He took the drive. "This will mean prison."

"Better than watching the country burn because I was too proud to admit I was wrong."

She left. He waited exactly sixty seconds, then walked out. The AFP units converged before he reached the fence.

"Evidence secured," he told the officer. "We need to get this to ASD. Now."

In the car, he opened his binder and wrote in block letters: **REID'S NETWORK IDENTIFIED. INFRASTRUCTURE COMPROMISE PRE-**

POSITIONED. COORDINATED ACROSS MULTIPLE CITIES.

Below it, smaller: *They planned this for months. We found it in hours.*

The officer looked at his notes. "You know what this means?"

"It means it's not an invasion," Noah said. "It's an inside job with outside help."

"That's worse."

"Or better. Inside jobs have trails. Trails have ends."

His phone buzzed. Reyes: *Southern window might open soon. Document everything. Paper backup.*

He looked at his binder—thick with truth now, evidence of patience versus chaos, planning versus discovery. They'd tried to break the country with templates and precision. But they hadn't counted on people who offered cake instead of capitulation, who played music instead of making speeches, who kept binders instead of trusting screens.

"Next stop?" the officer asked.

"Base," Noah said. "Then wherever the next cabinet needs checking."

The sun had reached the worst part of its arc. The city sweated and adapted. On the radio, someone was explaining why neighbors should share batteries. It sounded like civilization.

It sounded like winning, quietly, one decision at a time.

CHAPTER 13: HOUR 12:00
THE FARNHAM PROTOCOL

Sophie Kerr

The ABC newsroom at Ultimo had taken on the quality of a lighthouse in fog—everything beyond these walls uncertain, everything within focused on one job: keep the signal alive. Sophie Kerr stood at the assignment desk watching Sydney fracture through the windows while the city pretended noon was normal.

"Master Control says the encoder's gone from sulking to tantrums," Mo O'Hagan called from behind the equipment rack, a screwdriver clenched between his teeth like a cigarette he'd quit ten years ago. "AM's solid as my grandmother's marriage. FM's acting like a teenager. Digital's writing its will."

Sophie didn't look away from the crowd gathering on Harris Street. Two hours ago there'd been forty people. Now there were hundreds, and half their signs had the same grammatical tell she'd identified at dawn: *Turn it on, tonight* where it should read *Turn it on tonight*. The comma was deliberate—a signature, a tracking mechanism, a way to measure reach.

"Then we marry ourselves to the wrong century," she said, knotting duct tape around a length of coax that had seen better decades. "Mo, where's your ham setup?"

He patted the battered Yaesu FT-991A like it was a loyal dog.

"Right here. And before you mock my soldering, remember it survived the 2019 bushfire evacuations when everything else died."

The rooftop door banged open. Two producers in hi-vis vests that still had fold creases came down with a spool of wire and expressions of minor triumph. "Dipole's up," one said. "Stretched between the fire escape and that dubious pole on the west corner. Don't ask about workplace safety."

Sophie crouched by what they'd started calling the Analog Desk—the Yaesu, a Sangean portable that remembered when AM was king, a mess of adapters Mo had labeled with masking tape and optimism. The newsroom's background hum continued: keyboards like rain, phones on their last working lines, the particular exhausted tension of people who'd been on shift since midnight.

Outside, Sydney pretended to be normal. Buses growled past. A siren wound up six blocks away—ambulance, not fire, she'd learned to tell the difference twenty years ago when she'd started as a cadet. The Harbor Bridge carried its ant-line of traffic. The city hummed its electric baseline, the sound you only noticed when it stopped.

Which it was about to.

"Okay," she said, straightening. "We're going fishing for truth in an ocean of static."

They'd found an old laminated card in the emergency supplies—**HF Bands for Emergency Communications**—and taped it to the wall with the reverence reserved for ancestral knowledge. The greyline propagation marks showed when signals could leap continents, riding the edge between day and night.

"Start with the VK2 emergency net," Mo said, already turning the dial with safecracker concentration. "Forty meters, 7.110. If Sydney's hams are awake, they'll be there."

Static, then voices threading through like rescue ropes: *"VK2 portable at Parramatta... Macquarie Fields checking in... keep transmissions brief... we're not the only ones listening..."*

"God bless the amateur radio operators," Sophie murmured, keying the mic with practiced ease. She'd gotten her license during the millennium bug panic, never used it until today. "VK2 Sophie at Ultimo. ABC operational, monitoring emergency nets. What's the picture?"

A voice she recognized—Bob someone, ran the Hornsby club—came back immediately. "Sophie, good to hear you. We're getting reports of organized crowds at substations across the metro. Chants are coordinated, same timing. Also picking up Cairns and Brisbane nets— they're seeing similar."

"Any international traffic?"

"Mate's in Auckland says they've got crowds too, but police are playing Crowded House at volume and it's confusing everyone."

Sophie almost smiled. "Keep me posted. VK2 clear."

Mo had already shifted to the two-meter repeater network, the infrastructure the emergency services pretended didn't exist but knew would outlast the cellular towers. "Fire and Rescue net's clean. They're saying crowd at Mascot substation's growing. Someone's handing out signs."

Sophie lifted her desk phone—one of six lines still working—and dialed AFP media liaison. The officer who answered sounded like she'd been awake since yesterday.

"We see them," the officer said before Sophie could ask. "Mascot, Marrickville, Ultimo—your place too. We're treating it as organized but not immediately hostile. Though someone should tell them that surrounding critical infrastructure while the grid's failing isn't a great look."

Sophie moved to the window. The crowd below had swelled

again. A man with a milk crate and a megaphone was trying to start a chant. Behind him, three men in fresh hi-vis vests and identical backpacks stood like stage managers, not participating but watching everything. One kept touching his ear—comms piece, she'd bet her last coffee on it.

Her phone buzzed. Unknown number: *We can restore your broadcast. Approve encoder update. Help stability.*

She typed back what Reyes had taught the country: *Send cake.*

The reply came instantly: *Soon.*

"Linh," she called to the junior producer who'd been living on anxiety and determination since midnight, "can you pull social metrics?"

Linh's fingers flew across her tablet. "The comma tell you identified? It's in twelve languages now. German: *Schaltet es an, heute Abend.* Mandarin posts are using a specifically wrong particle. Spanish, French, Arabic—all the same grammatical signature. It's like they're using the same template with a localization error."

"Because they are." Sophie grabbed a marker and wrote on the whiteboard: **COMMA TELL = COORDINATED TEMPLATE**. Under it: **Track spread rate + origin points**.

The building's PA system crackled—Facilities, trying to sound routine. "Generator transfer in two minutes. Please save all work. We'll maintain emergency power to critical systems. Lifts will be offline. Stairwells remain lit."

"That's our cue," Mo said, hands already moving across the console. "If we lose the main encoder, we shift to the backup AM chain. The transmitter out at Prospect has its own power. Built in the seventies when people understood redundancy."

Sophie moved to Studio 2, the cramped backup booth they used for emergencies. The acoustic tiles were older than half the staff, yellowed like old teeth. The mixing desk was analog, built when vacuum tubes were giving way to transistors. But it worked. More importantly, it would keep working when everything digital forgot how to count.

She pulled on the headphones—heavy, uncomfortable, reliable. Through the glass, Mo gave her a thumbs up. They were live in twenty seconds. She thought about what Sydney needed to hear. Not panic. Not empty reassurance. Truth, delivered calmly.

Red light on.

"This is ABC Radio Sydney. It's midday, and if you're listening to this, it means you've already made the smartest decision of your day—you've found the frequency that won't leave you."

She kept her voice conversational, the tone she'd perfected over two decades of telling Sydney its own story back to itself.

"We're tracking organized gatherings at several substations across the city. If you're near one, particularly Mascot, Marrickville, or Parramatta, we ask that you maintain distance from the fences. The infrastructure you're looking at isn't a switch that someone's refusing to flip. It's a complex system that requires careful sequencing to restart safely."

Through the window, she watched the crowd surge slightly, then settle. Someone had started handing out bottles of water—staged charity for the cameras.

"We're also monitoring international emergency frequencies. This situation isn't unique to Sydney or Australia. Similar patterns are being reported across the Pacific region. The disruptions are coordinated, which means they can be countered through coordination."

Mo held up a piece of paper: **MASCOT HEATING UP - COUNCIL RESPONDING**

"If you're near the Mascot substation, you're about to hear some familiar music. The local council is providing what we'll call 'ambient crowd management.' We suggest you enjoy the soundtrack."

She could see it happening through the feeds Linh was monitoring on her tablet. A council truck with industrial speakers had pulled up to the Mascot crowd. The opening chords of *You're the Voice* erupted at competition volume. Half the crowd instinctively started singing. The man trying to lead chants looked personally offended that John Farnham had upstaged his revolution.

"For those just joining us, here's what we know: Darwin's hospitals remain on generator power, stable. The Prime Minister will address the nation at one o'clock on this frequency. If you have battery-powered radios, now's the time to find them. Share them with neighbors who don't."

The lights flickered—once, twice. The third time they dimmed to half power and stayed there. Through the window, Sophie watched the city's electric skeleton start to show.

Mo's hand was rotating urgently: wrap it up, technical difficulties incoming.

"We'll be back in five minutes with updates. In the meantime, remember: if you're at a dark intersection, it's now a four-way courtesy stop. If you have water, fill containers now. If you have elderly neighbors, check on them. This is Sophie Kerr, and we're not going anywhere."

Red light off.

"Encoder's dying," Mo said the moment she pulled the headphones off. "Digital chain's about to become abstract art. But AM's solid. The Prospect transmitter's running on diesel and spite."

Sophie moved back to the main newsroom. The crowd below had grown again, but something had changed. The organized core—the fresh hi-vis crew with their identical signs—were pulling back, replaced by genuinely confused locals who'd come to see what the fuss was about.

Linh appeared at her elbow with a printout. "ASD just sent this through the emergency channel. The comma tell matches code artifacts they found in Darwin. It's definitely a signature, probably for metrics—tracking how far their influence operation spreads."

Sophie felt the satisfaction of pattern recognition. Twenty years of journalism had taught her that the story was never what it claimed to be, but it always left fingerprints.

Her phone buzzed again. Another unknown number: *Final offer. Update now or lose broadcast capability.*

This time she didn't respond with cake. She typed: *We're Australian. We're used to everything trying to kill us. You'll have to do better than threatening our Wi-Fi.*

No response.

The building's PA crackled again. "Generator transfer commencing now."

The lights went out.

Emergency lighting kicked in—harsh, directional, turning the newsroom into a submarine. Through the windows, Sophie watched something extraordinary: Sydney's CBD dying in sequence. The Harbor Bridge lights extinguished south to north like someone running a finger along birthday candles. The Opera House screens went black in perfect order, as if the buildings were taking synchronized bows.

The city exhaled its electric breath.

Wynyard's underground entrance realized it was now just a hole. The buses stopped their chorus. The baseline hum Sophie had lived with her entire Sydney life... stopped.

"Grid down," Mo said quietly. He didn't need to elaborate.

Across the newsroom, monitors flickered between backup

power and death. The AM chain held—that beautiful, ancient, analog signal pumping out from Prospect like a heartbeat that refused to quit. But everything else was surrendering to black.

Sophie grabbed the emergency mic, the one hardwired to the AM transmitter. "This is ABC Radio Sydney. If your lights just went out, you're not alone. The CBD has lost grid power. This is a controlled shutdown to protect critical infrastructure. Your radio is now your lifeline. Stay with us."

She could see people in the street below pulling out phones, realizing they had no signal, no data, no connection except the voice coming through their radios—if they had radios.

"Mo," she said, "how long can Prospect run?"

"Diesel tanks are full. Three days if we're conservative. Longer if we cut overnight power."

"We don't cut anything. We stay on the air."

The Yaesu chose that moment to light up with traffic. International emergency frequencies were going mad. Sophie grabbed the headset and started scanning. Berlin: crowds with the same comma tell in German. Los Angeles: substations surrounded, identical timing. Singapore: organized groups with printed signs, same font, same message, different language.

"It's worldwide," she breathed. Then louder, for the newsroom: "This is coordinated across time zones. They're using the infrastructure attacks to drive people into the streets, then using the crowds to justify further shutdowns. It's a feedback loop."

The emergency lighting flickered. The generator was struggling.

Mo appeared at her shoulder. "Sophie, we might lose the building. But the Prospect transmitter will keep going. I can set up a remote feed from my car—it's got a mobile rig. We can broadcast from the parking garage if we have to."

She looked around the newsroom—her home for twenty years, the place where she'd learned to tell Sydney its own story. The young reporters were scared but working. The old hands were calm, having covered enough crises to know that panic was a luxury they couldn't afford.

"Set it up," she said. "Quietly. We don't abandon ship, but we prepare the lifeboats."

Her phone—one of the few still finding intermittent signal—buzzed with a text from a number she recognized. Kailana Reyes in Darwin:

Grid down was deliberate. We're protecting critical systems. Tell Sydney the switches aren't broken—they're being held by people who know the difference between fast and safe. Also, about those unknown numbers offering help? They're all NAT'd through Parliament House. Reid's friends are still playing.

Sophie read it twice, then typed back: *Sydney's listening. We're not going anywhere.*

She turned to face the newsroom—her people, her tribe, the ones who understood that journalism wasn't about being first, it was about being right when it mattered.

"Alright, everyone. The city's dark but not dead. The crowds are organized but we've identified their patterns. The infrastructure attacks are sophisticated but we've got people like Reyes holding the line. Our job hasn't changed—we tell Sydney what's happening, calmly and accurately. We are the voice in the dark."

She moved back to the emergency broadcast position. Through the window, Sydney was learning what it looked like without power. It was quieter than she'd expected. More beautiful too, in a terrifying way.

The Yaesu hummed beside her—that gorgeous old radio Mo had insisted on keeping, now their window to the world. Its display glowed green in the emergency lighting, steady as a heartbeat.

She keyed the mic for the forty-meter emergency net. "VK2 ABC Sydney. We're still here. Pass the word—Australia's still talking, even if the lights are out."

A chorus came back—voices from Brisbane, Adelaide, Perth, even a weak signal from Hobart. The amateur radio operators, the emergency services, the stubborn bastards with battery backups and diesel generators. The analog network that predated the internet and would outlast it.

Mo gave her the thirty-second signal. Back on air.

She pulled on the headphones and faced the microphone that connected her to a city learning to see in the dark.

"This is Sophie Kerr at ABC Radio Sydney. It's twelve-eighteen, and if you're just joining us, welcome to the most important radio broadcast of your life. We're going to get through this hour, then the next one, then the one after that. Together. Stay with me, Sydney. We're not going anywhere."

The red light glowed. The Yaesu hummed. Outside, a city of five million people was about to learn what community meant when the infrastructure failed but the people didn't.

The second hand on the battery-powered clock clicked toward 12:19. One minute at a time. That's how you survived when the world went dark.

That's how you won.

CHAPTER 14: HOUR 13:00 WITHOUT DECLARATION

Prime Minister Patricia Keating

The emergency studio hadn't been used since the 2019 bushfires. It still smelled of that smoke—ghost scent trapped in foam that had absorbed decades of Australian crisis. Patricia Keating stood at the threshold, remembering her mother's transistor radio during Cyclone Tracy, how the voice from this same building had said simply: *We're still here.*

Now it was her turn.

"Two minutes, Prime Minister," Kira Patel said, earpiece glowing blue in the dim emergency lighting. The building had switched to generators ten minutes ago. Through the narrow window, Canberra looked deceptively peaceful—government buildings standing like patients waiting for diagnosis.

Vale handed her a single page, text large enough to read if the lights failed entirely. The headings were verbs: **Prepare. Listen. Stay.** At the bottom, in Vale's precise hand: *Sydney CBD dark as of 12:18. Ultimo on generators. AM is the spine.*

"The southern window?" Keating asked.

"Woomera confirms it's available. Clean path through the orbital plane. But Prime Minister—"

"We don't perform tricks for applause. We save them for when we have no choice."

The red phone—landline, copper, older than most staff—rang once. Keating lifted it, knowing who it would be.

"Ma'am." Not Monash. A younger voice, female, stressed but controlled. Julia Ng from Darwin ops. "General Monash is at forward position East Arm. He asked me to confirm: full defensive posture maintained, hospital stable on generators, city dark by design. He'll be back on comms for your 1400 broadcast."

"Tell him his decision stands. Whatever he needs."

She hung up and found Reid's empty chair had been removed from the anteroom but its absence felt louder than its presence ever had. Eight hours ago he'd sat there arguing for centralized control, and all along he'd been—what? A traitor seemed too simple. A true believer in something worse.

The producer behind glass—young, competent, wearing a Midnight Oil t-shirt under his ABC vest—held up five fingers. Four. Three.

Keating moved to the microphone. It was older than her political career, a Neumann that had carried prime ministerial voices through wars, floods, fires. The foam windscreen was patched with gaffer tape that looked like stitches.

Two. One.

The red ON AIR light rose like a small sun.

"Good afternoon. This is the Prime Minister."

She let her voice find its register—not the parliamentary tone she'd perfected, but something older. The voice she'd used to read to her daughter during thunderstorms. The voice her mother had used during the White Australia debates, calm but immovable.

"If your power has failed in the last hour, your radio is now your lifeline. Sydney's central business district is experiencing controlled interruptions. This is deliberate. Our engineers are protecting the systems that keep you alive."

Through her earpiece, she could hear the faint echo of her own voice bouncing off a satellite, riding the AM carrier wave from the Prospect transmitter that Mo at Ultimo had sworn would outlast democracy.

"The lights that matter—operating theaters, intensive care, neonatal units—these remain powered. Your hospitals are breathing. Your water is flowing. These are the choices we're making: life before comfort, stability before speed."

She thought of Reyes in Darwin, hand on a panel, juggling hospital and base and desal plant. Of Sophie in Sydney, becoming the voice that held five million people steady. Of Monash, cut off from Canberra, making command decisions that would either save or damn him.

"We have invoked consultations with our allies under ANZUS Article Three. I want to be clear about what this means: we are coordinating our response, sharing intelligence, preparing options. We are not escalating. We are not declaring war on an enemy we cannot yet name with certainty."

Somewhere, she knew, Reid was in a secure cell, probably still smiling that cold smile. His network was being rolled up—the Marrickville warehouse, the pre-positioned devices, the parliamentary passes that had let saboteurs walk through their front door. But how deep did it go? How many Marcus Reids were there?

"You will hear rumors. You will see confident posts from people who claim there's a simple switch that could restore everything. This is false. There are thousands of decisions that must be made in precise sequence to safely restore power. Local engineers are making these decisions—not a computer in Canberra, not an algorithm, not politics. Human hands on local switches."

Vale slipped a note under her eyeline: *Mascot crowd dispersing. Farnham strategy successful.* Keating almost smiled.

"Some of you are standing at dark intersections. Treat them as four-way courtesy stops. Some of you have elderly neighbors who need checking. Some of you are boiling water on gas stoves, wondering what comes next."

She paused, let the silence carry weight.

"What comes next is this: we continue. We share batteries with neighbors. We keep emergency lanes clear for ambulances. We leave substation fences alone—they're not stages for frustration, they're boundaries that keep people alive."

The producer held up one finger—wrap it up.

"I will speak to you again at three o'clock, and again at five, and as often as needed. We will maintain this schedule until the crisis passes. In between, you'll hear from people whose names you don't know—engineers, emergency coordinators, the people doing the unglamorous work of keeping civilization running."

She thought of something her daughter had said during a childhood blackout: *It's like camping, but inside.* The absurdity and accuracy of it.

"One last thing. If you have a kettle and the means to boil water, make tea. Share it. I know this sounds ridiculous when I'm talking about infrastructure attacks and international coordination. But tea means you're still in a house that belongs to you, in a country that belongs to us. Civilization is a choice we make one cup at a time."

She leaned back slightly. The red light held.

"If you're in uniform today—police, medical, emergency services, military—thank you. If you're in hi-vis, keeping our infrastructure breathing, thank you. If you're checking on a neighbor right now instead of panicking, thank you. This is how we win—not with declarations, but with decisions."

The light clicked off. The producer gave a thumbs up that tried not to be emotional and failed.

Keating stepped out to find the anteroom had filled with people—Cabinet members who'd made it through failing transport, staff who'd been here since midnight, a handful of journalists who'd been in the building when lockdown began. They looked at her like she might have answers.

"Status," she said to Vale.

"Sydney CBD remains dark. Crowd control successful—music disruption at seven locations. Darwin maintaining defensive posture. JORN showing possible second wave forming northwest. US comms intermittent—they're dealing with Chicago, Detroit, Seattle simultaneously."

"Reid?"

"Preliminary interrogation suggests he genuinely believed he was preparing Australia for a 'managed transition.' He keeps using the phrase 'new architecture.'"

"Architecture," Keating repeated. The word sat in her mouth like stone. "He was remodeling while the house burned."

Hastings pushed through the crowd, still in yesterday's suit, tie long abandoned. "Patricia, we need to discuss Article Four conditions. The pressure—"

"The conditions remain unchanged." She counted them on her fingers, partly for him, mostly for the room. "Mass casualties on our soil. Attribution we can prove in court. An actual landing or boarding attempt. Or restored US capability to respond. Until one of those—"

"You're gambling—"

"I'm governing." She cut him off, then softened. "Peter, Article

Four is a door that doesn't close once opened. We invoke it when we can sustain it, not when we're scared."

Her personal phone—the one she'd forgotten existed—buzzed. Her daughter, safe at university housing: *Mum, we're sharing phone chargers and playing cards. It's like camping but inside. Love you.*

Keating typed back: *Stay exactly that smart. Love you too.*

"Prime Minister," the ABC producer appeared, Midnight Oil shirt now visible in full. "Sophie Kerr is asking for a line she can use if amateur radio operators ask about government response."

Keating thought about it. "Tell them this: 'We're still here. We'll be here tomorrow. The infrastructure can be rebuilt. The trust you're showing each other—that's the foundation.'"

Through the window, a maintenance crew was hand-pumping fuel into a generator, ordinary people doing extraordinary things by making them ordinary. That was the Australian way—not heroes, just humans who kept working when the systems failed.

"Ma'am," a comms tech appeared, face flushed from running up stairs that had no power. "Darwin's back on secure comms. General Monash for you."

She took the handset. His voice came through mixed with diesel generators and distant smoke.

"Prime Minister. Situation stable but evolving. I've maintained full defensive posture under my authority. I'll stand by that decision."

"Michael, you did what you needed to. You have my complete support. What's your assessment?"

"This isn't invasion, ma'am. It's something else. Reid was part of it but not all of it. The pattern suggests they want us to escalate, to invoke Article Four, to militarize the response."

"Why?"

"Because that would justify whatever comes next. They're not trying to beat us militarily. They're trying to make us reorganize ourselves."

Keating felt the truth of it settle in her bones. This wasn't war as previous generations understood it. This was forced evolution, crisis as catalyst.

"Hold your posture," she told him. "We don't give them the response they've scripted for us."

"Understood. And Prime Minister? Your broadcast—it's working. The tone, I mean. People need steady more than they need strong right now."

She hung up and turned to find the room watching her again. Ministers, staff, journalists—all waiting for something.

"We continue," she said simply. "Every two hours, I speak to the country. In between, the people doing the work speak. We don't catastrophize. We don't minimize. We tell the truth in words people can use."

Treasury raised a tentative hand. "Markets will expect—"

"Markets can expect what they like. Our priority order is: lives, infrastructure, stability, then markets. In that sequence."

She walked to the window. Canberra's government triangle looked peaceful, but she could see the emergency vehicles moving between buildings, the small groups of staff evacuating, the systematic shutdown of non-essential systems. It was like watching a body prioritize—brain, heart, lungs, letting the fingers go cold to keep the core alive.

"Kira," she said without turning, "set up the broadcast schedule. Every two hours, fifteen minutes maximum. Rotate the infrastructure ministers through—water, power, transport, health. Give people voices to associate with systems."

"Yes, Prime Minister."

"And find out if Sophie Kerr can do a segment on amateur radio protocols. Those operators are holding secondary comms together. They deserve recognition."

She thought about the briefcase in her office, Article Four sitting in its envelope like a loaded weapon she refused to draw. Reid had wanted her to use it. The pattern of attacks seemed designed to force it. Which meant not using it was itself a form of resistance.

Her phone showed 13:24. In Darwin, Reyes would be checking her generators, reading diesel levels like vital signs. In Sydney, Sophie would be fielding emergency nets, turning chaos into information. Across the Pacific, similar scenes in different languages—the comma tell spreading like a signature, infrastructure failing in coordinated waves, crowds with printed signs and suspicious timing.

But also: neighbors sharing batteries. Councils playing John Farnham to disperse crowds. Amateur radio operators building invisible bridges across the dark. The human infrastructure that no amount of planning could sabotage because it wasn't planned—it simply emerged when needed.

"We're going to win this," she said, still facing the window.

"How do you know?" Hastings asked.

She turned back to the room. "Because they're trying to make us be something we're not. And Australians are world champions at refusing to be what we're told."

A few people actually laughed—small, tired, but real.

"Alright," she said. "Back to work. We've got a country to hold together with AM radio and tea. Our ancestors would be proud and appalled in equal measure."

The clock showed 13:28. Thirty-two minutes until she'd face the microphone again. In those minutes, Sydney would stay dark, Darwin would hold its perimeter, and across the continent, people would make the small choices that looked like nothing but were everything: checking neighbors, sharing resources, choosing patience over panic.

The war that wasn't a war continued.

Australia continued back.

CHAPTER 15: HOUR 14:00
OUR OWN NOON

Lieutenant Kailana Reyes

The Darwin plant room had become a cathedral of decisions—every switch a prayer, every gauge a confession. Kailana Reyes stood before the main panel with one palm pressed against the metal, feeling the sixty-hertz heartbeat of a city trying not to die.

"Time's lying," Batty said from behind her, the young signals tech whose hair stood up like he'd been personally offended by electrons. "PTP drift is accelerating. Someone's trying to become our clock master, and they're doing it with forged certificates that are technically perfect."

On the wall, three clocks showed three different times. The analog one—mechanical, honest—read 14:00. The digital display insisted it was 14:03. The GPS receiver couldn't decide and kept flashing between 13:58 and 14:05.

"If we lose time sync—" Batty started.

"We lose sequential control." Reyes finished. "Protection relays fire out of order. Generators try to sync to different frequencies. The hospital's life support systems start arguing about when to breathe."

Through the reinforced window, Darwin steamed in its afternoon stupor. Smoke from the morning's fuel depot attack had settled into a brown line across the harbor. The city she'd blacked out six hours ago stayed dark, patient as a held breath.

The copper phone rang—one sharp note. "Reyes."

"NICU." The voice was controlled panic trying to sound professional. "Our ventilator alarms are stuttering. The machines think they're seeing power fluctuations that aren't there. Something about timestamp conflicts?"

"Two minutes," Reyes said, already moving.

She grabbed the emergency kit she'd assembled at dawn—a rubidium frequency standard older than her career, borrowed from the F-18 maintenance shop because someone twenty years ago had been too sentimental to throw it out. The box hummed with atomic precision, the only honest time-keeper left in a building full of sophisticated liars.

"Time cart," she told Batty. "We're going Victorian. Physical distribution of a local time signal. No network, no spoofing, just copper and truth."

They loaded the rubidium box onto a maintenance cart along with an IRIG-B timecode generator and enough coaxial cable to reach the hospital's critical systems. Batty grabbed a distribution amplifier. Reyes added a label with a Sharpie: **TIME CART 1 - IF LOST, RETURN TO REYES - SHE WILL CRY.**

The AEMO controller—a woman named Patricia who'd been awake so long her Queensland accent had dissolved into something universal—looked up from her switching schedule. "You're creating your own time domain?"

"We're going to be our own noon," Reyes said. "Darwin runs on Darwin time. Let the rest of the world argue about when 'now' is."

Patricia's laugh had no humor in it. "The grid control software won't like that."

"The grid control software is currently telling me that effect is preceding cause and that the hospital used power three minutes before requesting it. I'll take hurt feelings over dead babies."

She started the isolation sequence, fingers moving with the muscle memory of someone who'd drilled this scenario but never believed she'd use it. Cut the NTP servers. Disable PTP announce packets. Block the GPS timing input that was currently insisting it was simultaneously tomorrow and yesterday.

A window popped up on the management console: *Approve timing correction? Source: Parliamentary Standards Authority.*

"Oh, you bastards," she whispered. Parliamentary Standards Authority didn't exist. But the certificate was perfect, the signing chain immaculate, the timestamp—

The timestamp was from next week.

She photographed it, then killed the process with extreme prejudice.

"Hospital," she told Batty. "Move."

They rolled through corridors that smelled of diesel and determination. The backup generators thrummed their mechanical mantras. Everyone they passed had the same expression—exhausted competence, the look of people doing their third job because the first two had failed.

At the hospital's main distribution frame, the power engineer—Marcus, whose uniform had transcended dirty into archaeological—met them with visible relief.

"NICU's on isolation power but the transfer switches are arguing. They can't agree on when the last switchover happened, so they keep trying to re-do it."

Reyes connected the rubidium standard to the IRIG-B generator, then started running coax to the critical distribution panels. The time signal—one pulse per second, boring and perfect—began flowing through copper that didn't care about certificates or networks or someone in Canberra trying to redefine reality.

"This is stone age," Marcus said, watching her work.

"Stone age worked for fifty thousand years," Reyes replied, terminating another connection. "Silicon age barely made it to fifty."

The NICU ventilators stopped their stuttering. The transfer switches agreed on a version of reality. In the critical care ward, machines that had been jazz musicians became metronomes again.

Her phone buzzed. A message from Sophie in Sydney: *Lost grid at 12:18. CBD dark. Running on generator and spite. How's your time?*

Reyes typed: *We're writing our own. Darwin is our own noon.*

"Ma'am," Batty said, monitoring his spectrum analyzer. "I'm seeing coordinated announce packets hitting every network interface we haven't physically disconnected. They're trying five different time domains simultaneously."

"Let them." She sealed the last connection and stood. "We're not listening to the world anymore. We're—"

An explosion—not close, but heavy enough to feel through the floor. Southwest. The port direction.

The copper phone on the wall rang before she could reach it. Julia Ng from ops: "Kamikaze drone into Berrimah substation. Transformer's gone. East suburbs losing power in cascade."

"Redirect through Palmerston tie," Reyes said, mental map updating. "Drop commercial load first, residential second. Keep water treatment online."

"Already moving. But Lieutenant—that substation powered the main cellular towers."

Mobile phones across the room began dying as their last tower connections failed. The city that had already lost internet now lost its voice.

Except for one thing.

"ABC's AM transmitter is on the Winnellie feeder," Reyes said. "That stays up no matter what we lose. Sophie needs to keep talking."

She moved back to the plant room at a run that pretended to be a fast walk. The main display showed Darwin fragmenting—dark zones spreading like ink, islands of light where hospitals and water treatment held on, the port a careful constellation of essential systems.

The management console tried one more time: *System time is incorrect. Allow remote correction?*

This time Reyes didn't just refuse. She yanked the network interface out physically, dropped it on the concrete floor, and brought her boot down with prejudice. The crack was deeply satisfying.

"From now on," she announced to the room, "any system that wants to tell us what time it is can get in line behind our atomic clock. We trust copper and physics. Everything else is propaganda."

Patricia looked at the switching schedule that had just become fiction. "Without network time protocol, we'll have to coordinate everything by voice. Like it's 1970."

"Then we party like it's 1970," Reyes said. "Get me every qualified operator who can read an analog gauge. We're going manual."

The next explosion was closer. Through the window, a fresh column of smoke rose from what had been a cellular relay station. Someone was systematically cutting Darwin's ability to coordinate.

But they'd made one mistake. They'd assumed everything ran on networks. They'd forgotten about people like Mo in Sydney with his ham radios, about copper phone lines that remembered when digital was science fiction, about engineers who'd learned their trade when computers were suggestions, not commandments.

About atomic clocks that didn't care about certificates.

Reyes looked at the rubidium standard humming on its cart. One pulse per second. Honest. Indifferent. Immune to lies.

"Alright," she said to the room. "Darwin runs on Darwin time. Every critical system gets a physical time feed. No networks, no negotiations. We are our own noon until the world remembers how to count."

The lights flickered—once, twice—then steadied. Somewhere, a generator had made a decision. Somewhere else, a protection relay had fired in the correct sequence because it was listening to an atomic heartbeat through copper wire.

Outside, Darwin endured its isolation. Inside, Kailana Reyes put her palm back on the panel and felt the city breathing in time with itself, ignoring the chaos of a world that had forgotten when now was.

"Hospital?" she asked Patricia.

"Steady. NICU perfect. Operating theaters synchronized."

"Water?"

"Pumping in sequence."

"Base?"

"Running fifteen seconds fast, but consistently fast."

"Then we hold," Reyes said. "We hold until the world catches up to Darwin time."

Patricia glanced at her screen. "Woomera says they have

options if we need them. Something about commercial redundancy."

"Save it," Reyes said. "We trust copper first, space second."

The clock on the wall—mechanical, spring-driven, older than the building—ticked toward 14:30. It didn't care about networks or certificates or someone trying to redefine reality from a Parliament House NAT.

It just marked seconds, one after another, like footsteps walking away from chaos.

CHAPTER 16: HOUR 15:00
MUSIC AND MAGNETS

Sophie Kerr

The generator had found its rhythm—a diesel heartbeat that made the building feel like it was breathing. Sophie Kerr stood at the newsroom window watching Sydney learn what three hours without power meant. Below, Harris Street had thinned to the genuinely confused and the professionally committed. Half still carried signs with the comma tell: *Turn it on, tonight.*

"Mascot's heating up," Mo said from the radio desk, one ear covered. "Emergency net says two hundred people now. Someone's handing out water bottles and portable chargers—but only to people with the right signs."

"Staged charity," Sophie said. "Get me vision if anyone's still got battery."

The Yaesu crackled with cross-talk. Perth checking in—they still had power but crowds were forming preemptively. Brisbane reporting organized groups at seven substations. Auckland saying their cops were now playing Dave Dobbyn at volume and confusing everyone on purpose.

Sophie's phone—one of three in the building still finding intermittent signal—buzzed with another unknown number: *Last chance. Approve encoder update for restoration.*

She didn't bother responding. They'd tried this script six times.

The answer wasn't changing.

"Listen to this," Mo said, patching in the forty-meter band. A British voice, tired but clear: *"London emergency net to all Commonwealth stations. Comma pattern confirmed in Manchester, Birmingham, Leeds. Someone's using the same template globally. It's definitely a tracking signature."*

Sophie grabbed her notebook and circled what she'd written three hours ago: **COMMA TELL = COORDINATED TEMPLATE**. Under it she added: **Global. Same timing. Same error.**

Linh burst through the stairwell door, tablet clutched like a life preserver. "AFP just called. They want you to know something before they move on Mascot. There are devices under the substation cabinets. Magnetic, about the size of a can of Coke. They're not bombs—they're something else."

"What kind of something else?"

"The kind that makes protection relays lie about when things happened. Time bombs, but for sequence, not explosion."

Sophie felt the pattern crystallize. The infrastructure attacks, the time protocol drift Reyes had been fighting, now physical devices to compound the confusion. Make the systems argue about when to do things, and they'd tear themselves apart without any actual damage.

"Mo, give me thirty seconds of dead air, then I'm live."

She moved to the emergency broadcast position. Through the window, she could see the Mascot crowd in the distance, a dark mass around the substation fence. Someone had brought a megaphone. Someone else had brought a ladder.

Red light on.

"This is Sophie Kerr at ABC Sydney. If you're near the Mascot substation, or any substation, I need you to listen carefully. AFP have discovered devices designed to disrupt the protection systems. These aren't switches someone is refusing to flip—these are sabotage devices that will make restoration harder, not easier. The crowds gathering at these sites are preventing their removal."

She could hear the fury in her own voice and pulled it back.

"In the next few minutes, you're going to hear music at some of these locations. Local councils are providing what we'll call ambient crowd management. I suggest you enjoy it. Dancing is optional but encouraged."

Mo held up a note: **IT'S STARTING**

Through the emergency net, she could hear it beginning. First Mascot—*You're the Voice* erupting from a council truck's speakers at competition volume. Then Marrickville—*Working Class Man* loud enough to rattle windows. Parramatta got *Khe Sanh.* Liverpool, inexplicably, got *Eagle Rock* which started an immediate arms-and-eagle situation that destroyed any attempted organization.

"This is brilliant," Linh whispered, watching the feeds on her tablet. "They can't maintain a coordinated chant when half the crowd is doing the Eagle Rock."

Sophie watched the Mascot crowd fracture in real-time. The organized core—the ones with fresh vests and identical signs—tried to maintain discipline. But Australians presented with Farnham at volume had only one cultural response, and it wasn't political.

Her phone rang. Not a message—an actual call. She almost didn't answer, then saw it was a Darwin number.

"Sophie?" Kailana Reyes, sounding exhausted but vindicated. "We found them too. The cans. They're networked, trying to broadcast false time stamps. Every substation in Darwin had them. We're pulling them now."

"Same here. Music's working to clear the crowds."

"Music?" Reyes laughed—short, sharp. "We went with water sprinklers and CO2. Your way sounds more fun."

"Any word from Monash?"

"He's holding the perimeter. Lost comms with Canberra so he's making unilateral decisions. The kind that save you or sink you."

The line crackled and died. Sophie tried calling back but the network was gone again.

Through the window, she saw something that made her grab binoculars. At the Mascot substation, while the crowd was singing and dancing, three AFP officers in tactical gear were methodically working along the fence line. One had what looked like a magnetic wand. Another carried evidence bags. The third was photographing everything.

They were pulling small black objects from under cabinet lips, from behind junction boxes, from anywhere metal met metal. The cans. Physical proof that this wasn't about restoration—it was about preventing it.

"Mo, patch me through to the emergency net. Wide as you can make it."

The radio network opened—ham operators from Cairns to Hobart listening in.

"VK2 ABC Sydney with traffic for all stations. AFP recovering physical sabotage devices from substations. Magnetic attachment, designed to disrupt protection systems. If you have engineers trying to restore power, have them check for cans, boxes, anything that shouldn't be there. These are preventing restoration, not protests."

The net exploded with confirmations. Melbourne had found them. Adelaide. Even Hobart, where there hadn't been crowds, had discovered three devices pre-positioned.

Sophie went back on AM. The red light steadied her.

"Sydney, this is what we now know. The infrastructure attacks included physical devices designed to prevent restoration. These are being removed as I speak. The crowds at substations—many genuinely concerned citizens, but organized elements using them as cover. The comma tell we identified? It's worldwide, same error in dozens of languages, a signature to track the operation's spread."

She paused, let that sink in.

"We also know this: the music is working. Councils across Sydney are now deploying what we're calling the Farnham Protocol. If you hear Australian rock at volume near critical infrastructure, enjoy it. It's the sound of your country refusing to follow someone else's script."

Through the window, the Mascot crowd had fully transformed. What started as organized protest had become an impromptu street party. Someone had brought out a barbecue. The AFP officers worked unmolested, pulling can after can from the substation equipment while people did the Eagle Rock ten meters away.

Mo held up another note: **Darwin back on secure line**

Sophie grabbed the phone. Not Reyes this time—Julia Ng from ops.

"Ms. Kerr, General Monash wanted you to know—the devices you're finding are the same as ours. Same manufacture, same configuration. This was pre-positioned weeks ago, maybe months."

"Reid's network?"

"Almost certainly. We're rolling up the Sydney cell now. Marrickville warehouse full of equipment."

The line crackled with distance and failing infrastructure.

"Tell Monash we're holding Sydney with AM radio and Australian music. Whatever works."

"He said you'd say that. He also said—" The line died completely.

Sophie looked at the clock: 15:27. Three and a half hours since the grid collapsed. The city below was adapting—she could see it in the way people moved. Less panic, more purpose. At intersections without lights, cars had developed an organic flow. Neighbors were checking on each other. The human infrastructure was emerging.

"Sophie," Linh said quietly. "Look at this."

On her tablet, a social media post from someone still finding signal: a photo of the recovered cans, laid out on a tarp. Dozens of them. Each labeled with location and time found. The comment thread was exploding—not with conspiracy theories, but with engineers explaining exactly how these would prevent restoration.

The narrative was shifting. The infrastructure attacks were being exposed not as government conspiracy but as sabotage. The crowds were seeing they'd been used.

Sophie went back on air for the half-hour update.

"This is ABC Sydney. It's three-thirty on a Monday afternoon that none of us will forget. The power remains out, but the truth is emerging. Physical sabotage devices have been recovered from substations across the city. The organized crowds are dispersing. The restoration can begin—carefully, systematically, the way it has to be done."

She thought of Reyes in Darwin, trusting copper and atomic clocks. Of Monash, cut off from command, making decisions that would echo for decades. Of Keating in Canberra, refusing to escalate into someone else's war.

"We're going to get through this hour, then the next one, then the one after that. With radio and music and the peculiar Australian talent for turning crisis into community. Stay with us, Sydney. We're not going anywhere."

The red light clicked off. Through the window, the Mascot crowd was now fully committed to a spontaneous street party. Someone had started a conga line. The AFP officers had finished their work and were actually smiling.

The sabotage devices sat in evidence bags—small, black, malevolent, and defeated.

The city was dark, but it was dancing.

CHAPTER 17: HOUR 16:00 UNKNOWN-12

Major General Michael Monash

The ops floor had developed the specific quiet of people who'd been awake too long to waste words. On the main screen, Darwin's wounds showed in neat categories—power districts like a chess board with half the squares removed, the harbor's fuel slick drawing its accusation across the water, and a new icon that made Monash's jaw tighten: a white triangle labeled **UNKNOWN-12** drifting sixty nautical miles northeast.

"Talk to me about the triangle," Monash said.

Julia Ng pulled up the feed from NORFORCE Patrol Three—shaky phone footage from a dune on Cobourg Peninsula. A long white hull pretending to be helpful. No nets deployed. Crew moving with the wrong kind of purpose for fishermen.

"AIS says she's the *Lucky Dragon*, home port Makassar," Ng said. "But her track for the last six hours is a figure-eight that would make any actual fisherman broke and seasick."

"And her friends?"

"Two more hulls in loose formation. One's broadcasting as a tuna boat that's allergic to tuna grounds. The other isn't broadcasting at all."

Monash studied the track patterns. Twenty years of watching

the Arafura had taught him the difference between fishing and loitering. These weren't fishing.

The secure phone rang—or tried to. The connection came through like someone shouting through soup.

"Wedgetail has eyes on your triangle," the RAAF controller said through static. "Heat signatures all wrong. Deck cargo under tarps that's organized like someone cared about weight distribution. We're seeing antenna farms they forgot to hide."

"How confident?"

"Confident enough that we're burning fuel to keep looking."

Monash turned to the room. "Right. Unknown-12 is now our primary interest. But we're not going to make it famous yet."

He picked up the copper line to Canberra, got three seconds of Vale's voice, then nothing. The backup satellite link showed ERROR. The emergency HF radio gave him what might have been Keating saying "your discretion" or might have been atmospheric noise having opinions.

"Sir," Hargreaves said from radar, "P-8 from Edinburgh requesting permission to investigate. They can be on-station in forty minutes."

"Approved. Tell them to be boring. We watch, we don't wave."

Julia Ng's fingers were already moving. "Creating maritime area of interest. What do you want to call it?"

Monash thought about bureaucratic naming conventions, then thought about what would make sense to a tired operator at three in the morning.

"KANGAROO ONE. Simple box, twelve-mile radius from Unknown-12's current position. Observe and report only."

On his desk, the coin his father had carried through Vietnam sat untouched. The maturing general, about to make another decision without Canberra's input because Canberra had become a rumor.

"Sir," the intelligence officer said, sliding photos across the desk. "These just came from Shark Two."

Handheld pictures, blown up and grainy, but clear enough. The white hull's deck arrangement. Tarps lashed over rectangular shapes. A crane that belonged on a construction site, not a fishing boat. And in one corner, barely visible, the edge of what looked like a launch rail.

"Containerized system," the Army major said quietly. "Same type the Iranians have been shopping around. Bolt it to any deck, instant navy."

"How instant?"

"Fifteen minutes from decision to launch, if they've practiced."

Monash looked at the clock: 16:14. Full dark in four hours. If they were going to move, they'd wait for night. Which meant he had a window.

"P-8, give me everything. Thermal, magnetic, electronic. I want to know what brand of cigarettes they're smoking."

The Poseidon crew came through clearer than Canberra had in hours. "Copy. Going dark and nosy."

Julia pulled up another screen. "RAN has Cape Byron available. She's doing fisheries patrol, but she's got a boarding party and a gun that works."

"Vector her to shadow. No closer than twelve nautical. Tell her to look uninterested."

"Sir," Hargreaves interrupted, "I'm getting scatter suggesting more toys warming up. Not launched, but... spinning. Like they're doing preflight."

The pattern was clear. Morning had been probing—test the defenses, measure response times. Now they were positioning for something bigger. But what? Another swarm attack? Or something worse?

His secure phone tried again. This time he got ten seconds of Keating's voice: "—your authority—defensive measures—no attribution—"

Then nothing.

"I need options," Monash said to the room. "Assume Unknown-12 is hostile. Assume they're carrying containerized launch systems for drones. What stops them without starting a war?"

The Navy liaison raised a hand. "Mission kill. Take out the crane and rails but leave the hull floating. They can't launch but they're not sinking. Plausible deniability."

"With what?"

"Williamtown has a two-ship on ready-five. Small diameter bombs, GPS guided. Surgical."

Monash thought about Sienna Crossman, who'd cleared Newcastle's sky eight hours ago. Good hands on the stick. The kind of precision they'd need.

"Draft the order," he said. "Don't send it. Options only."

The P-8 crew cut through the static: "Definite containerized launch system. Four tubes minimum, maybe eight. Crane is powered and warm. We're also seeing... sir, there's a control van. Air-conditioned, lots of antennas. That's your command node."

"Can you identify origin?"

"Negative on markings. But the configuration matches known exports from—" The line dissolved into static.

Everyone knew what came after "exports from." But nobody said it. Attribution was Keating's decision, if Keating could be reached.

"Sir," Julia said quietly, "if they launch at dark, that's less than four hours."

"I know."

He looked at the board again. Darwin dark but breathing. Hospital generators holding. The reef of burnt fuel depot. And sixty miles northeast, a white hull full of questions preparing answers nobody wanted.

The copper phone rang. Not Canberra—Reyes.

"General, we've isolated Darwin time from the network. We're our own noon. If you need synchronized operations, we'll have to coordinate by voice like it's the seventies."

"Can you give me clean timing for a potential strike package?"

A pause. "You're thinking about hitting the boat."

It wasn't a question.

"I'm thinking about stopping launch rails from being rails."

"I can give you a ten-second window where our defensive systems won't see friendlies as threats. But General—we can't deconflict with anyone else. If there are other assets up—"

"There won't be. This would be surgical. If it happens."

"Your call," she said. "I'll have the window ready."

He hung up and found the room watching him. The weight of command without communication. The loneliness of decisions that would be judged by people who weren't here.

"Alright," he said. "KANGAROO ONE goes live. We watch Unknown-12 like it owes us money. Cape Byron shadows. P-8 maintains coverage. Ready strike package but do not load weapons. We're building options, not commitments."

"And if they start launching?" the Army major asked.

"Then we stop them launching. No attribution, no headlines,

just physics preventing physics."

Julia's phone lit up. She listened, paled slightly. "NORFORCE reports Unknown-12 is recovering something from the water. Small boat, moving fast."

On screen, the track showed the white hull had stopped its lazy loop and was now moving with purpose. Southwest. Toward the oil platforms. Toward the shipping lanes.

Toward Darwin.

"Time to weapons range if they maintain speed?"

"Three hours to launch range for medium UAVs. Two hours for the swarm controllers."

Monash picked up the coin, rolled it once between his fingers—his father's habit when thinking became decision.

"Signal Williamtown. Ready-one, pilots to cockpits. Tell them it's probably nothing but be ready for something."

He looked at the clock: 16:31. In Canberra, Keating would be preparing for another broadcast, trying to hold the country together with AM radio and carefully chosen verbs. In Sydney, Sophie would be reading emergency nets and turning chaos into information.

Here in Darwin, he was about to prepare to sink something that wasn't technically an enemy from a country they hadn't named in a war nobody had declared.

"Sir," Hargreaves said, "Unknown-12 just went active on radar. She's painting the sky."

"She's looking for us."

"No sir," Hargreaves corrected. "She's making sure we see her looking. She wants us to know she's aware."

The game had changed. They weren't hiding anymore.

"KANGAROO ONE rules of engagement," Monash said

clearly. "If Unknown-12 or associates launch anything that threatens Australian infrastructure or lives, we stop the launch capability. Minimum force, maximum precision. No crew quarters, no engine rooms. Mission kill only."

Julia was already typing. "Sending to Williamtown."

"And Julia?" Monash added. "Find me five minutes of clear comms with Canberra. I need to tell the PM what I'm about to possibly do."

"I'll try, sir. But—"

"I know. We're on our own."

Through the window, Darwin's afternoon was fading toward an evening nobody wanted. Sixty miles away, a white hull full of wrong answers was sailing toward a question.

The coin sat still in his palm. His father had carried it through three tours, never spent it, never explained why. Michael understood now. Some currency was for keeping, not spending.

"Back to work," he said. "We've got three hours to be ready for whatever they think we're not ready for."

CHAPTER 18: HOUR 17:00
RAILS TO NOWHERE

Flight Lieutenant Sienna Crossman

The F-35's cockpit was already warm when Sienna Crossman dropped into the seat. Seventeen hours since this started, five hours since she'd last been up, and now the horizon was pulling her back into the sky.

"Viper One, you're hot in two," the crew chief yelled over the Pratt & Whitney's awakening growl. "Overwatch has your target picture. Weapons release authorized on confirmation."

She pulled the straps tight—shoulders, waist, legs—until the jet became an extension of her spine. Helmet on, visor down, the world narrowed to displays and decisions.

"Viper Two, radio check," she called.

"Two's up," Nikki Parnell responded, all business now. "Standard load?"

"Negative. Four Small Diameter Bombs each. GPS and laser. We're doing surgery, not demolition."

The cockpit displays bloomed with data. On her left screen, the target: sixty nautical miles northeast, a white hull labeled UNKNOWN-12 that had spent the afternoon pretending to fish while painting Darwin's sky with targeting radar.

"Tower, Viper flight ready for immediate."

"Cleared immediate departure, runway zero-eight. Overwatch has your discrete frequency."

She pushed the throttle. The Lightning rolled forward with the particular eagerness of a machine built for one thing. Nose light, main gear up, Darwin falling away beneath. The late afternoon sun painted everything gold except the smoke still rising from the morning's fuel depot attack.

"Viper flight, Overwatch," came the E-7 controller's voice—calm, female, probably hadn't left her scope in twelve hours. "Picture: Unknown-12 bears zero-four-five for sixty, angels two thousand, speed four knots, aspect south. P-8 confirms containerized launch rails under tarps. Crane is active. They've recovered personnel from small boats. Cape Byron shadowing at twelve nautical. ROE is mission kill only—rails and crane, no hull, no crew spaces."

"Copy. No headlines, just physics."

She banked northeast, keeping the throttles conservative. No afterburner, no aggressive climbs. If Unknown-12 had decent sensors, she wanted to look like a routine patrol until she didn't.

"Two, tactical spread. I'll take the rails, you get the crane mechanism."

"Two."

The ocean scrolled beneath—Cobourg Peninsula's mangroves, then open water the color of old steel. On her tactical display, Unknown-12 appeared as a triangle with data tags: length, beam, probable displacement. The P-8's sensor pod had done its work—infrared showing hot spots where machinery lived under tarps.

"Overwatch, Viper. What's the deconfliction status?"

"Darwin's running isolated time protocol. They've opened a ten-second window at 17:12 local where their defensive systems won't prosecute friendlies. Miss that window and NASAMS might have opinions."

"Ten seconds?"

"Lieutenant Reyes says she can give you fifteen if you ask nicely, but she's juggling a city with atomic clocks and copper wire."

Sienna smiled behind her oxygen mask. Reyes—the engineer keeping Darwin's infrastructure breathing by force of will. They'd never met, but she felt like she knew her through the crisis.

Twenty miles out, she started the attack sequence. Weapons bay doors opened with a whisper. Four SDBs showed ready. The targeting pod locked onto Unknown-12's deck and started building the precision points—not just GPS coordinates but specific aim points on specific structures.

"Viper One, Overwatch. Unknown-12 just increased speed to eight knots. Aspect changing to southwest. They're heading for the shipping lanes."

Or Darwin. Or both.

"Two, we prosecute on my mark. Single pass, no second looks."

Through the targeting pod, she could see Unknown-12 clearly now. White hull, rust at the waterline, crew moving with purpose. Four containerized launch tubes barely concealed under blue tarps. The crane amidships, painted yellow like construction equipment. A van on the aft deck that had to be the command node.

This wasn't a fishing boat. This was a weapon pretending to be innocent.

"Range fifteen miles. Designating."

She assigned the forward rails to SDB one and two, the aft rails to three and four. The bombs' computers accepted the targeting with electronic satisfaction—they lived for this kind of precision.

"Viper Two, confirm crane designated."

"Two's sweet. Slew bearing and hydraulics. She won't lift anything heavier than regret."

Ten miles. Five. The ocean filled her peripheral vision.

"Unknown-12 active on X-band," Overwatch warned. "They see you."

"Let them look."

She pickled the first pair. The SDBs fell away, deployed their wings, and began their glide—not dumb ballistics but thinking munitions, adjusting their path for wind, checking their GPS, comparing what they saw in infrared to what they expected.

Below, she saw crew running. Someone pointing up. Too late.

The first two SDBs hit the forward rails simultaneously. No massive explosion—these were penetrators with minimal explosive. Just enough to turn launch rails into modern art. Metal shrieked, twisted, became unusable.

She pickled the second pair. They found the aft rails with the same precision.

"Viper Two, in hot."

Nikki's bombs separated, glided, struck. The crane's head separated from its body like a bad relationship ending. The slew bearing that let it rotate became several pieces that no longer agreed on their purpose.

Through the pod, Sienna saw crew scrambling with firefighting equipment. Small fires where hydraulic fluid had met hot metal. But no massive damage, no hull breach, no bodies in the water.

Mission kill. Not murder.

"Viper flight off target. Damage assessment?"

The P-8 crew came through immediately: "Rails are scrap metal. Crane is modern art. Launch capability zero. They're containing minor fires. No casualties observed. Hull integrity maintained."

"Overwatch confirms. Unknown-12 is now just a boat with a bad deck arrangement and trust issues."

Sienna climbed back to patrol altitude, checking fuel. Plenty to get home, with reserve for contingencies. Through her six-o'clock camera, she could see Unknown-12 falling behind, smoke wisping from its deck, no longer a threat to anything but its insurance company.

"Viper flight, RTB."

They turned southwest, back toward Williamtown, back toward a base that would want debriefs and paperwork and explanations. But first, just flying—the ocean golden in the late sun, the turbine humming its one note, the satisfaction of precision applied precisely.

"Overwatch, Viper. Pass to Darwin control—target neutralized, no collateral, no headlines."

"Copy. Lieutenant Reyes says 'clean timing, cleaner shooting.'"

Sienna thought about the engineer she'd never met, holding Darwin together with determination and atomic clocks. About Monash, making command decisions without Canberra because Canberra had become a ghost. About Keating, somewhere trying to hold a nation together with AM radio.

"Tell her we're even," Sienna said.

The Australian coast appeared—brown and green and achingly familiar. Below, Newcastle's lights were coming on in patches as Sophie's reporting had promised they would. The grid healing itself slowly, carefully, one substation at a time.

Her radio crackled with Williamtown tower, routine vectors, the ordinary business of coming home. But as she descended through five thousand feet, Nikki's voice cut through on their tactical channel.

"Lead, Two. Check your six camera."

Sienna looked. Unknown-12 had stopped trying to contain the deck fires and was now dead in the water. But more interesting—two more white hulls had appeared, converging on it. The other players, coming to collect their wounded piece.

"You seeing this, Overwatch?"

"We see it. They're recovering personnel. Looks like they're abandoning Unknown-12."

So it was over. The platform was neutralized, the threat ended, the mission complete. But those other hulls would disappear into international waters, become different names, different flags, and the game would continue.

"Viper flight, tower has you on approach. Cleared straight in runway two-six."

She lowered the gear, felt the jet configure itself for landing. Below, the familiar geometry of Williamtown—the hardstands, the hangars, the crew already waiting.

Touchdown was smooth as silk. The jet rolled out, turned off, found its place in the line. The canopy rose and evening air rushed in—eucalyptus and jet fuel and the particular smell of a base that hadn't slept in twenty-four hours.

The crew chief was already on the ladder. "Clean jets, ma'am. Not a scratch."

"Clean mission," she replied, unstrapping. "Rails that won't launch, crane that won't lift, and nobody we have to notify."

He grinned. "My kind of war story."

She climbed down, legs stiff, shoulders aching where the harness had held her. Across the ramp, Nikki was already out, helmet under her arm, talking to the intelligence debrief team.

Sienna's phone—which had been off for the flight—buzzed with accumulated messages. One from an unknown Darwin number: *Whoever flies Viper One—thank you for the clean work. Rails neutralized, no wet footprints. This is how we win. —K. Reyes*

She typed back: *Just returning the favor. You kept the timing, we kept it simple.*

The message sent, riding whatever thin connectivity the base had managed to maintain. Somewhere in Darwin, an engineer would read it between juggling transformers and arguing with atomic clocks.

The sun was setting properly now, painting everything the color of endings. But Williamtown was very much alive—jets turning, crews moving with purpose, the base ready for whatever the night would bring.

"Debrief in ten, ma'am," someone said.

"Copy."

She took one last look north, toward where Unknown-12 was now probably settling lower in the water, its mission as dead as its crane. No attribution, no headlines, no war declared. Just physics applied to physics, precision answering provocation.

The job.

CHAPTER 19: HOUR 18:00 NEW ARCHITECTURE

Prime Minister Patricia Keating

The Cabinet room had taken on the quality of a submarine running out of air. Six hours since the grid collapsed, two hours since secure communications with Darwin died, and now the international board showed new fires: Washington dark, Beijing silent, London requesting assistance they knew wouldn't come.

Patricia Keating stood at the window watching Canberra pretend toward evening normalcy while her secure phone delivered fragments of a world reorganizing itself.

"Prime Minister," Vale said, entering with papers that looked like they'd been printed on three different machines as backups failed. "Confirmation via maritime surveillance. Unknown-12 is dead in the water. Rails destroyed, crane inoperative. No casualties, no attribution. Monash executed perfectly."

"Without my authorization."

"With your pre-stated intent. He made the command decision when comms failed."

Keating turned from the window. Around the table, what remained of the crisis cabinet—some in person, others via failing video links, one calling from his car because the ministry building had been evacuated.

"Update," she said.

ASD's deputy, via a connection that kept pixelating: "We've recovered seventeen devices from Sydney substations. Same configuration as Darwin. The key finding—" He held up a circuit board. "These were manufactured at least six months ago. The firmware has version control dating to last year. This wasn't opportunistic. This was planted and waited."

"Reid's network?"

"His and others. We're finding parliamentary passes issued to foreign nationals as 'technical consultants.' The Marrickville warehouse has equipment for at least a hundred more devices. But Prime Minister—here's what matters."

He held up a printout, the comma tell circled in red.

"This grammatical error appears in twelve languages, always the same position, always paired with specific timing. It's not random. It's a tracking signature. They're measuring influence spread like a medical trial. Which cities respond, which don't, what percentage of population engages."

Treasury, barely audible through static: "Markets are down eighteen percent. Without clear attribution—"

"We don't attribute what we can't prove in court," Keating said. "Being right isn't enough. Being legally right is what prevents wars."

The door opened. Hastings entered with a face that preceded its news.

"NATO's invoked Article 5."

The room stopped breathing.

"Based on?" Keating asked.

"Coordinated infrastructure attacks across seven member states. They're calling it an act of war against the alliance."

Keating felt the weight of Article IV in her briefcase, heavier now. If NATO was mobilizing, the pressure to invoke ANZUS would become crushing.

"U.S. position?"

"Unclear. Some states have gone dark. Federal government is... distributed. Pentagon says they need seventy-two hours to restore command integrity."

Her phone rang. Not the secure line—her personal mobile, which shouldn't have signal. The caller ID showed her daughter.

"Thirty seconds," she told the room and stepped into the hall.

"Mum?" Her daughter's voice, stressed but trying not to be. "The student news is saying we're at war. That you're about to declare—"

"We're not at war. We're responding to infrastructure attacks. Are you safe?"

"Yes. We're in the residence common room. Someone brought a radio. We heard your broadcast."

"Good. Stay together. Share resources. I'll call when I can."

"Mum? That minister they arrested—Reid—his office sent us all internship offers last month. Paid. Generous. Lots of us applied."

Keating's blood chilled. "Did you?"

"No. Something felt wrong about it. But Mum—at least twelve did."

"Names. Send me names. Now."

She ended the call and walked back in to find the room arguing.

"—NATO activation changes everything," the Foreign Minister was saying via a connection that made him look like abstract art. "We have to—"

"We have to nothing," Keating cut him off. "NATO's decision is NATO's decision. Our conditions for Article IV remain unchanged."

Vale slid another paper across—fresh intelligence, still warm. "P-8 surveillance shows three more vessels converging on Unknown-12's position. They're recovering equipment and personnel. International waters. No legal intervention possible."

"So they got their probe and their data," Keating said. "They tested our responses, measured our capabilities, and now they're cleaning up."

"Prime Minister," Hastings said, and she heard the generational weight in his voice—old soldier, Cold War thinking, binary enemies. "Every hour we delay—"

"Every hour we delay, we maintain options. The moment we invoke Article IV, we're locked into escalation. They want that. The pattern is clear—provoke declaration, justify response, reorganize the region while everyone's shooting."

Her secure phone managed ten seconds of clarity. Monash's voice: "—perimeter holding—expecting probe at twenty-two hundred—Tiwi beaches—"

Then nothing.

"He's expecting another probe tonight," she told the room. "Coastal, probably small boats, testing our beach defenses."

The wall screen flickered and updated. A single line of text from Woomera: SOUTHERN WINDOW AVAILABLE ON REQUEST.

Keating looked at it for a long moment. Their ace—a laser uplink through space-based relay that couldn't be jammed or spoofed. But using it would reveal capability, show cards they might need later.

"Not yet," she said.

"Patricia," Hastings said, using her first name like a weapon. "If boats land tonight—"

"If boats land tonight, Monash will stop them. If they establish a beachhead, that triggers Article IV. But probing isn't landing. Testing isn't invading."

Through the window, she could see the maintenance crew had given up on one generator and were manually pumping fuel into another. The Parliament House that had hosted Reid's network was running on emergency lighting, throwing angular shadows.

"Prime Minister," Vale said quietly, "Sophie Kerr's about to broadcast from Sydney. She's requesting guidance on public messaging."

Keating thought about Sophie in her powerless newsroom, holding five million people steady with AM radio and competence. About Reyes in Darwin, orchestrating infrastructure with atomic clocks and copper wire. About Sienna Crossman, who'd just performed surgery on a threat without creating a headline.

"Tell her this," Keating said. "We're not at war. We're at work. The infrastructure attacks are being countered. The sabotage devices are being removed. Every hour we maintain services is an hour we win."

The clock showed 18:27. In less than four hours, boats would probably probe the Top End beaches. The pattern suggested escalation—test, probe, push until something broke or someone declared war.

"Cabinet position," she announced. "We maintain Article III consultations. We prepare all defensive measures. We do not escalate. We do not attribute without evidence that would stand in international court. We win by enduring, not by declaring."

"And if they land?" Hastings pressed.

"Then Article IV triggers automatically and you can have your war. But not before. Not on suspicion. Not on fear."

She picked up the briefcase, felt the weight of the envelope inside.

"I broadcast again at nineteen hundred. Until then, we hold. Darwin holds its perimeter. Sydney restores its grid carefully. We document everything. And we don't give them the war they're trying to provoke."

She left them arguing and walked to the small studio where the microphone waited. Through her earpiece, she could hear Sophie Kerr in Sydney, voice steady as stone: "This is hour eighteen. We're still here. So are you."

The rhythm of crisis had established itself—two steps forward, one step sideways, no steps back. They would make it through this hour, then the next, then the one after that.

With or without declaring war.

CHAPTER 20: HOUR 19:00
PROBABILITY TO CERTAINTY

Major General Michael Monash

The ops floor had shifted into its nineteenth hour with the particular exhaustion of people who'd forgotten what sleep tasted like. Coffee cups accumulated like evidence. Someone had brought in sandwiches six hours ago; they sat untouched, developing personalities. On the main screen, Darwin's defense perimeter glowed in neat concentric rings—NASAMS batteries, RBS-70 positions, the beaches where NORFORCE had melted into landscape with the patience of people who belonged to the land before it belonged to a map.

Michael Monash stood behind Julia Ng's station, watching her work three keyboards simultaneously while conducting two phone conversations in a mixture of English and Mandarin. The coin in his pocket—his father's, from Vietnam—sat heavy and untouched. Some currency you didn't spend.

"Sir," Hargreaves called from radar, voice carrying the specific tension of someone seeing something turn from possible to probable. "Multiple small contacts, north-northeast, approximately forty nautical out. Moving in coordination."

"Speed and heading?"

"Twelve knots, bearing two-two-zero. Direct line to Tiwi beaches."

Monash looked at the clock: 19:03. Three hours earlier than expected. They were accelerating the timeline, probably because Unknown-12's neutralization had left them exposed. The white hull was now being stripped by its friends in international waters, but its mission—probe, test, measure—continued.

"How many?"

"Six to eight surface contacts. Small signatures. Could be fishing boats, could be ribs, could be both pretending to be neither."

The secure phone to Canberra rang—or tried to. What came through was Keating's voice filtered through static and failing satellites: "Michael—assessment—"

"Multiple contacts inbound to Tiwi. Three hours out at current speed. Probable landing probe."

"—authority remains—defensive measures—" The line died completely.

He turned to the room. Twenty-three people, most on their second wind, some on their third coffee. The weight of command without communication sat clean on his shoulders.

"Right. We assume hostile intent. Julia, flash to NORFORCE—eyes on Tiwi beaches, Snake Bay priority. They're to observe and report until my word. No independent action."

"Copy." Her fingers flew across keys that had lost half their letters to wear.

"RBS-70 teams to forward positions. I want overlapping coverage from high-water mark to one kilometer inland. If anything flies that isn't ours, we introduce it to gravity."

The Army major was already on his radio, voice calm and precise. In the field, teams would be moving through darkness that had become familiar, setting up kill zones in places their grandfathers had defended against different threats.

"Sir," the intelligence officer said, sliding fresh imagery across the desk. "P-8 managed these before losing illumination."

Grainy infrared photos. The lead vessel was a thirty-footer with too many antennas and not enough fishing gear. Behind it, smaller boats in formation. One carried what looked like a communications dome. Another had rectangular shapes under tarps that weren't trying very hard to hide.

"Landing craft," Monash said. It wasn't a question.

"Or probing force. Test our beach response, measure reaction times, identify gaps."

He picked up the copper line to Darwin facilities. Reyes answered on the first ring, sounding like she'd been mainlining caffeine and determination.

"General."

"Beach probe inbound. If this escalates, I need the coastal detection net online. Can you feed it?"

"I can give you fifteen minutes of coverage, but it'll brown out East Arm. Pick your priority."

"Lives over lights."

"Copy. Also, General—we found something. The devices pulled from substations? They're not just time disruptors. They're mapping our restoration sequences. Learning how we bring things back online."

"So they can break it better next time."

"Or prevent us from fixing it at all."

He filed that away—another piece of the pattern. Not just attack but study. They were being examined as much as assaulted.

"Sir," Julia interrupted, "Wedgetail's requesting authorization to illuminate. They can paint the inbounds without going active."

"Approved. Let them know we see them."

On the tactical display, an E-7A Wedgetail's track appeared—lazy oval at thirty thousand feet, sensors reaching out like fingers to touch the approaching boats. Within seconds, the contacts sharpened from probable to certain.

"Eight vessels confirmed. Lead element is steel-hulled, likely command. Six ribs in formation. One trailing element—bigger, slower. Possible supply or recovery."

"Time to beach?"

"Two hours forty minutes to Tiwi. Two hours to Cape Don if they divert."

Monash studied the approaches. Tiwi had the beaches but also the population. Cape Don was isolated but closer to the fuel infrastructure. Snake Bay split the difference—good landing, minimal civilians, access to the Stuart Highway if they got inland.

"They'll take Snake Bay," he said. "Best compromise for a probe."

The secure phone tried again. This time he got Julia Ng's counterpart in Canberra—Vale's voice threading through static: "PM wants assessment without escalation. Article Four conditions unchanged unless actual landing—"

"Understood. We defend the beaches without creating headlines."

The line died again. He was getting used to the isolation, the way command felt when you couldn't phone a friend.

"NORFORCE, Shark Three," came through the tactical net. An elder's voice, patient as stone. "Movement on the water. Lights running dark. Can hear engines—sounds like Yamahas, maybe Mercs. Moving with purpose."

"Distance from shore?"

"Twenty k and closing. We're in position above Snake Bay. Good sight lines. The boys are painting their faces and remembering their grandfathers."

Despite everything, Monash almost smiled. NORFORCE—the North-West Mobile Force—was largely Indigenous, recruited from the communities they protected. They knew this land in ways satellites never would.

"Keep your boys safe, Shark Three. Eyes only until I call it."

"Copy. But sir? If they land, we'd prefer to handle it quiet. Our country, our way."

"Negative. If they hit sand, we light them up proper. No heroes, no spears. Modern solutions to modern problems."

A pause. "Copy. But the offer stands."

Julia looked up from her screens. "Cape Byron reports she's diverted from fisheries patrol. Can intercept in ninety minutes."

"Tell her to shadow at distance. Visible but not aggressive. We want them to know we have options."

The Navy liaison cleared his throat. "Sir, if these are special forces probing, they'll have rehearsed. They know our response times, our coverage gaps. They're not here to invade—they're here to measure."

"Then we give them something to measure," Monash said. He turned to the room. "Full defensive posture, but we make it look routine. No panic, no rush. They're watching our reaction as much as testing our beaches."

The intelligence officer raised a hand. "Recommend we stand up deception measures. IR strobes at false positions, radio chatter on frequencies we know are compromised. Make them think we're somewhere we're not."

"Do it."

Outside, Darwin's evening had settled into its humid embrace. The smoke from the morning's attacks had finally dissipated, leaving only the smell—burnt fuel and foam retardant, the perfume of modern conflict. Through the reinforced windows, he could see the harbor lights, the careful constellation of infrastructure they'd fought to protect.

"Sir," Hargreaves said, tension climbing in his voice. "Airborne contact launching from lead vessel. Small, slow, heading inland."

"UAV. They're scouting the beaches."

"Do we take it?"

Monash weighed the choice. Shoot it down, reveal defensive positions. Let it fly, concede intelligence.

"Let it look. But launch our own. I want eyes on their eyes."

A Ghost Bat UAV rolled out from its shelter at RAAF Darwin, autonomous systems spinning up. Within minutes it would be airborne, shadowing the enemy drone, learning what it looked at, mapping what it cared about.

"Sir, new development," Julia said, phone pressed to her ear. "Sydney's reporting organized crowds returning to substations. Same signs, same timing. It's coordinated with our naval approach."

The pattern crystallized. Probe the beaches, distract with civil unrest, measure the response when forces were divided. Classic insurgent tactics scaled to nation-state level.

"Get me Sophie Kerr."

The connection took three attempts. When it came through, Sophie's voice carried the exhaustion of someone who'd been talking for nineteen hours straight.

"General?"

"Sophie, crowds are coordinated with a beach probe here. They're trying to divide attention. Can you—"

"Already on it. The Farnham Protocol rides again. Every council truck with speakers is rolling. We're about to turn Sydney into an involuntary musical."

"Good hands," he said, then caught himself. The phrase had become their reflex, their shorthand for competence under pressure.

"You too," she replied, and the line went dead.

On the screen, the approaching boats had formed into a clear assault pattern—lead element with the command vessel, two columns of ribs, the trailer maintaining distance. Classic amphibious approach, except these weren't marked military vessels. They were ghosts, deniable, the kind of force that could disappear into fishing fleets if challenged.

"One hour to beach," Hargreaves announced.

"All stations, this is Commander JTF North," Monash said into the command net. "Probable hostile approach to northern beaches. Rules of engagement: warning shots authorized upon attempted landing. Disable boats if possible, detain personnel if they reach shore. No lethal force unless fired upon. We defend without headlines."

He looked at the coin in his palm—hadn't remembered taking it out. His father had carried it through three tours, '68 to '71, when the world last tried to reorganize this region. Different enemy, same questions. When was a probe an invasion? When did defense become war?

"Sir," the intelligence officer said quietly, "if they land and we repel them, that's clear. But if they land and establish any kind of position, even briefly—"

"Article Four triggers," Monash finished. "Which might be

exactly what they want."

The room fell into the rhythm of preparation—quiet voices, purposeful movement, the particular energy of people who'd trained for this but hoped never to use it. Outside, NORFORCE teams were becoming part of the landscape. RBS-70 operators were checking their missiles for the third time. Somewhere in Canberra, Keating was probably staring at the same tactical feed, making the same calculations.

"Forty-five minutes to beach," Hargreaves called.

The Ghost Bat's feed appeared on screen—infrared imagery of the approaching boats. He could see personnel on deck, weapons, the nervous movement of people about to do something they couldn't take back.

"Sir," Julia said, "southern window is available if you need to speak to—"

"No," Monash cut her off. "We save that card. This is our problem until it isn't."

He stood behind the tactical display, watching eight dots crawl toward a line in the sand that meant more than geography. The Tiwi beaches had seen landings before—Japanese reconnaissance in 1942, Indonesian fishermen for centuries before that. But this was different. This was probing the boundary between old wars and new ones, between what you could prove and what you knew.

"Thirty minutes to beach."

"Light them up," Monash ordered. "All sensors active. Let them know we see them."

The tactical display exploded with energy as every radar, infrared sensor, and electronic eye turned toward the approaching boats. It was the modern equivalent of chambering a round—audible, visible, unmistakable.

On the lead boat, someone made a decision.

"Aspect change," Hargreaves called. "They're turning."

Not away. Parallel to shore. Still approaching but obliquely now, feeling the edge of territorial waters like a blind man feeling for a wall.

"They're looking for gaps," the intelligence officer said.

"They won't find them," Monash replied. "NORFORCE, you tracking?"

"Like watching ants at a picnic," Shark Three replied. "They're nervous. Lead boat's doing something with their dome."

"Electronic warfare. They're mapping our emissions."

The boats continued their parallel track, twelve nautical miles out—international waters, technically legal, tactically provocative. They were learning without landing, probing without providing cause.

"Sir," Julia said, "they're transmitting. Burst communication, satellite uplink."

"Sending the data home."

Twenty minutes passed. The boats maintained their track, gathering intelligence, measuring responses. Then, as suddenly as they'd appeared, they turned north.

"They're withdrawing," Hargreaves announced, surprise in his voice.

"No," Monash corrected. "They're finished. They got what they came for."

The room deflated slightly—relief mixed with anticlimax. They'd prepared for battle and gotten reconnaissance.

"Stand down from immediate posture," Monash ordered. "Maintain surveillance. They might come back."

But he knew they wouldn't. Not tonight. They'd learned what they needed—response times, sensor coverage, defensive positions. The next probe would account for all of it.

"Sir," the intelligence officer said, studying the recordings, "this was professional. Military professional."

"I know."

"That's attribution."

"That's inference. We need evidence that stands in court, not just in this room."

The secure phone rang—clear for once. Keating's voice, controlled but tired: "Michael."

"They probed but didn't land. We lit them up, they turned away. No shots fired, no violations we can prove."

"So we're still at Article Three."

"Yes, ma'am."

A pause. Then: "Good work."

She hung up. Monash looked at the tactical display—empty now except for the withdrawing boats and Cape Byron shadowing at distance. Darwin had held for another hour. Australia had avoided war for another night.

But the pattern was clear. Each probe more sophisticated, each test more precise. They were being measured for something bigger.

"Rotation in thirty," he told the room. "Eat something that lies about being food. Sleep if you can. They'll be back."

He put the coin back in his pocket, his father's talisman unspent.

The war that wasn't quite a war continued its patient approach.

CHAPTER 21: HOUR 20:00
PAPER TRAIL

Noah Tan

The AFP evidence lockup at Darwin police headquarters had the particular smell of truth documented—paper, ink, the metallic tang of electronic devices sealed in Faraday bags. Noah Tan stood at the examination table, twenty hours without proper sleep making everything feel like it was happening underwater, but his hands were steady as he laid out the chain of connections.

"This one," he said, pointing to a circuit board photographed from sixteen angles, "matches the Marrickville workshop output. Same solder patterns, same component sourcing, same firmware fingerprint."

The AFP detective—Sarah something, too tired for surnames—leaned over the display. "How long would it take to plant all these?"

"Months. Maybe a year. You'd need access during maintenance windows, knowledge of which substations matter most, and people who could pass background checks."

"Reid's network."

"Reid's network was the inside part. This," Noah gestured to the collection of devices, photos, and documentation spread across three tables, "this needed external support.

Manufacturing, logistics, coordination."

His phone buzzed. Unknown Darwin number—but he recognized the style. Reyes, texting from whatever terminal still worked: *Found another can at Berrimah backup. Timestamp shows it was placed eight months ago. How deep does your paperwork go?*

He typed back: *Following money trail. Parliamentary consultancy contracts. Will have names within hour.*

The detective picked up one of the magnetic cans, turned it over behind its evidence bag. "We pulled forty-three of these across Sydney and Darwin. If they'd all activated—"

"The grid wouldn't know when anything happened. Protection systems would fire randomly. Generators would try to sync to different frequencies." Noah pulled out his battered ring binder, now thick as a phone book with documentation. "It's not about destroying infrastructure. It's about making it impossible to trust."

Through the window, Darwin's night was the peculiar dark of a city running on selected generators. Points of light where hospitals breathed, darkness where suburbs waited. The raids on two more safehouses had yielded seventeen arrests, but Noah knew the arithmetic—more devices than people caught. The network was bigger than they'd found.

"Mr. Tan," a voice from the doorway. ASIO this time, the kind of suit that suggested Canberra even in Darwin's humidity. "The template analysis you provided. We need the linguistic breakdown."

Noah flipped to the section he'd tagged with yellow sticky notes. "The comma tell appears in twelve languages, always after the same word position. But here's what matters—it's not a translation error. It's deliberate. A tracking signature to measure spread."

He showed them the printouts from social media, highlighting the pattern. "Beijing standard simplified Chinese. Moscow institutional Russian. Tehran Farsi with specific dialect markers. But all using the exact same grammatical structure, just localized."

"Attribution," the ASIO officer said.

"Inference," Noah corrected, unconsciously echoing Monash. "We can prove coordination. We can't prove origin."

His laptop—the ancient one without wireless that he trusted more than his own reflection—dinged with a completed search. Financial records from a parliamentary database that someone had forgotten to take offline.

"Got you," he whispered.

On screen: seventeen consultancy contracts, all legitimate on paper, all paying foreign nationals as "technical advisors" to various parliamentary offices. The amounts were reasonable, the work descriptions plausible. But the dates...

"They all started thirteen months ago," he said, highlighting the pattern. "Different offices, different stated purposes, but all initiated within the same two-week window."

The detective was already photographing the screen. "That's planning."

"That's infiltration."

Another text from Reyes: *Time attacks accelerating. Someone's trying to become our clock master before midnight. Can your evidence help us predict next move?*

Noah looked at his documentation, then at the map of Darwin on the wall with its constellation of red pins marking device locations. There was a pattern there, something about the placement, the timing...

"They're not random," he said suddenly. "Look—the devices cluster around specific infrastructure. Not just critical systems, but the restoration nodes. They mapped our recovery procedures."

He grabbed a marker and started connecting pins. "If Darwin blacks out here, we restore through this substation. But there's a device. So we route around to here—another device. Every fallback has been compromised."

"Jesus," the detective breathed.

"They didn't just want to break things. They wanted to prevent fixing them."

The ASIO officer was already on his phone, relaying the discovery. Noah could hear fragments—"restoration routes compromised... need alternative sequences... manual bypass only..."

Through the window, a helicopter passed low, spotlight sweeping the harbor. The news had been cycling through the same footage for hours—Unknown-12 dead in the water, the Mascot crowds dispersing to John Farnham, Keating refusing to say the word "war."

Noah's phone rang. Sophie Kerr from Sydney.

"Noah, I need something quotable about the devices for the nine o'clock bulletin. Technical but not terrifying."

"They're synchronized disruption devices," he said, finding the words as he spoke them. "Designed to confuse infrastructure about timing and sequence. We've found them, we're removing them, and we're restoring services through alternative paths."

"Perfect. Also, that shed you found? The 3D printing setup? AFP found two more in Sydney. Same equipment, same templates."

"They prepared for this like a theater production. Multiple understudies for every role."

"Speaking of theater," Sophie said, "crowds are reforming at substations. Night shift. But the councils are ready with speakers. We're about to blast *Working Class Man* at volume across western Sydney."

Despite everything, Noah smiled. "The Farnham Protocol."

"The Barnes Variation. Got to go."

She hung up. Noah turned back to his evidence, but the detective was holding up a new report.

"Coastal surveillance just picked up small craft approaching from the northeast. Again."

Noah checked his watch: 20:23. The morning probe had been reconnaissance. The afternoon had been measurement. This would be...

"They're going to try to land," he said. "That's the escalation pattern. Probe, measure, commit."

The ASIO officer looked at him sharply. "Based on?"

Noah flipped through his binder to the section where he'd mapped the timeline. "Every action has been six to eight hours apart, each more aggressive. The infrastructure attacks created distraction. The civilian crowds divided attention. Now they test physical boundaries."

He thought of the fresh hi-vis vests in the warehouse, the pre-printed signs, the rehearsed nature of everything they'd found. Months of preparation for twenty-four hours of execution.

"I need to get this to Monash," he said, gathering the critical documents.

"Transport's down," the detective said. "Roads are blocked for emergency vehicles."

Noah looked at the evidence—weeks of work compressed into pounds of paper. Then at his laptop with its searchable database. The physical trail that courts would need and the digital summary that commanders could use.

"I'll walk," he said.

"It's six kilometers to JTF headquarters."

"Then I'll walk fast."

He loaded the essentials into a backpack—the financial records, the device analysis, the pattern recognition that showed escalation. His ring binder went into a waterproof bag. The laptop into another.

"Mr. Tan," the ASIO officer said, "that intelligence is—"

"Useless if it doesn't reach the people defending the beaches."

He left before they could argue. Outside, Darwin's heat wrapped around him like a wet blanket that had been left in a sauna. The darkness was peculiar—not the full black of a blackout but the selective shadow of a city running on decisions. Emergency lighting at intersections. Generators humming behind critical buildings. The hospital complex glowing like a statement of priorities.

Noah started walking, then jogging. The backpack bounced against his spine. Six kilometers through a city under siege, carrying evidence that might—might—help predict the next move.

His phone buzzed. Reyes again: *Southern window might activate soon. Document everything. Physical backup for when digital fails.*

He thought about the months of preparation Reid's network had invested. The sophistication of the attack. The coordination across time zones. This wasn't opportunistic. This was orchestrated.

But they'd made one mistake. They'd assumed Australia would respond predictably—panic, escalate, invoke Article IV, militarize the response. Instead, Keating had held steady. Monash had defended without declaring. Sydney had turned protests into sing-alongs.

And people like Noah had done what Australians did—documented everything, followed the money, kept careful records in ring binders that couldn't be hacked.

Three kilometers in, a ute pulled alongside. ABC logo on the door, Mo from Sydney's newsroom behind the wheel.

"Need a lift?"

"What are you doing in Darwin?"

"Flew up this morning to establish backup broadcast. Sophie thought you might be walking around with important papers. She was right."

Noah climbed in. The ute smelled of coffee and determination.

"JTF headquarters?"

"Yeah. Monash needs to see the patterns."

Mo drove through the selective darkness, navigating by memory and emergency lights. "Sophie says to tell you the comma tell has gone viral in reverse. People are posting corrections, pointing out the error. The influence operation is being turned into grammar lessons."

"Trust Australians to weaponize pedantry."

They reached JTF headquarters as the clock touched 20:45. The building blazed with emergency lighting, generators roaring defiance. Noah grabbed his evidence and ran for the entrance.

Inside, organized chaos. He could hear Monash's voice from the ops floor—calm, decisive, preparing for what everyone knew was coming.

Noah had evidence. Darwin had defenses. Australia had stubborn refusal to follow the script.

The night's test was approaching across dark water.

CHAPTER 22: HOUR 21:00 UNOPENED ENVELOPE

Prime Minister Patricia Keating

The secure communications room had been renamed "the submarine" by staff who'd been underwater for twenty-one hours. No windows, recycled air, and the particular desperation of people making decisions in isolation. Patricia Keating stood before the wall display showing Australia like a patient's chart—critical systems in green, failures in red, and Darwin pulsing amber like a wound that wouldn't quite heal.

"Prime Minister," Vale said, entering with Marcus Reid's preliminary interrogation transcript. "You need to see this."

Keating took the papers, still warm from the printer. Reid's words, spoken three hours into custody, precise as scalpels:

"You think this is about China or Russia or America. It's not. It's about the architecture of the next century. The old alliances are theater. NATO, ANZUS, Five Eyes—they're nostalgic institutions pretending relevance. The world is reorganizing into resource blocks and technology dependencies. Australia can either accept its position in the new hierarchy or be dissolved into components."

"He's lecturing from a cell," Hastings said from across the table, his old soldier's face carrying twenty-one hours without sleep like a badge. "We should—"

"Read the next part," Vale interrupted.

Keating found the highlighted section:

"By 22:00 tonight, you'll face a choice. When those boats land—and they will land, Prime Minister—you'll invoke Article IV because you'll have no choice. The Americans won't come. They can't. Their grid is more compromised than yours. And when Australia stands alone, declaring war on an enemy it can't name, the region will reorganize around you, not with you."

The wall clock showed 21:03. Fifty-seven minutes until Reid's prediction.

"Arrogant bastard's probably right," Hastings said. "The boats Monash is tracking—they're not fishing vessels. We all know what they are."

Keating set the transcript down carefully, like placing a loaded weapon on a table. Through her earpiece, she could hear fragments of Monash's operations—military brevity codes, coordinates, the controlled tension of forces preparing for contact.

Her personal phone buzzed. Her daughter: *Mum, twelve students from Reid's internship program just got arrested. They were trying to access university infrastructure. Same devices you found. How deep does this go?*

She typed back: *Deep enough. Stay inside. Stay together.*

"Prime Minister," the intelligence director appeared on screen, his Canberra office visible behind him, emergency lighting making everything angular. "We've completed analysis of the Marrickville workshop. The equipment, the templates, the devices—they match seizures in Berlin, Chicago, Singapore. This is global, coordinated, and rehearsed."

"Attribution?"

"The money trails to shell companies in three jurisdictions. The hardware has components from seven countries. The software has fingerprints from at least four different intelligence services, possibly deliberately mixed to prevent attribution."

Keating felt the weight of it—not just an attack but a new kind of warfare where proving who pulled the trigger mattered less than the chaos created.

"Ma'am," Vale's earpiece lit up. She listened, paled. "Darwin. The boats have accelerated. Monash estimates beach contact in thirty minutes."

The room's attention snapped to the tactical display. Eight boats in attack formation, approaching Snake Bay at speed. The ghost icons of NORFORCE positions dotted the beach approaches. RBS-70 markers showed anti-air coverage. Everything ready for a fight nobody wanted but everyone expected.

Keating picked up the secure phone—or tried to. Static, fragment of voice, then nothing.

"Southern window?" she asked Vale.

"Woomera says ready on your word. But Prime Minister—"

"Once we reveal that capability, everyone knows we have it."

"And the commercial implications?" Hastings asked. "Let the oligarchs have their moment when it comes," Keating said. "Sometimes private infrastructure serves public good."

The door opened. Foreign Minister Park entered with the kind of face that preceded diplomatic catastrophe.

"Beijing just issued a statement," she said. "They're expressing 'concern about Australia's unilateral military actions' and warning against 'provocative responses to maritime navigation.' They're pretending those boats are civilian."

"While knowing they're not."

"While knowing we know they know."

Hastings stood, his patience finally depleted. "Patricia, we're out of time. The boats will land. Our forces will engage. People will die. If we don't invoke Article IV now, we'll be doing it under fire in forty minutes."

Keating walked to the wall display, studied Darwin's defenses. She thought of Monash, isolated from command, preparing to repel boarders with whatever authority his rank and situation provided. Of Reyes, keeping the city's infrastructure breathing through sheer determination. Of Sophie in Sydney, holding five million people steady with nothing but AM radio and competence.

"Get me Reid," she said.

"What?"

"Bring him here. Now."

Vale hesitated. "Prime Minister, that's—"

"That's an order."

The wall display updated with an unexpected addition—a social media feed that had found its way through dying networks. A single post from @elonmusk: *Southern sky still clear. Starlink is stubborn.*

Reid's smile flickered. "You can't maintain independent communications indefinitely."

"We don't need indefinitely. We need tonight. And apparently," Keating gestured to the screen, "we have friends with infrastructure."

Twelve minutes later, Reid entered in restraints, flanked by AFP officers. His suit was gone, replaced with detention center grey, but his smile remained—cold, certain, like someone watching their own script perform.

"Patricia," he said, using her first name like a weapon. "Running out of time?"

"You said twenty-two hundred. You said they'd land. You

knew because you helped plan it."

"I helped prepare Australia for its transition. There's a difference."

She studied him—this man who'd sat in Cabinet, who'd had access to their deepest secrets, who'd betrayed not just trust but the concept of trust itself.

"What do they want?"

"What everyone wants. Resources. Position. Compliance." He shifted, chains clinking. "But mostly they want you to declare war. Because a declared war justifies intervention. Peacekeeping. Restructuring."

"By whom?"

His smile widened. "Does it matter? Beijing, Moscow, Delhi—they're all preparing to help stabilize Australia once you've admitted you can't. Article IV is your suicide note."

"And if we don't invoke it?"

"Then Australians die on beaches while their Prime Minister watches."

Keating felt the trap's teeth—invoke Article IV and justify intervention, or don't and accept casualties. Either way, Reid's architects won.

Unless.

"Vale," she said, not looking away from Reid. "Signal Woomera. Activate southern window. Full spectrum."

Vale hesitated. "Prime Minister—"

"Do it."

Reid's smile flickered. "You can't maintain independent communications indefinitely."

"We don't need indefinitely. We need tonight."

The wall display changed. A new icon appeared—a satellite constellation linked by laser paths, labeled only SW-ACTIVE. Within seconds, clear communications flooded back.

Vale leaned close. "The Musk people are asking for acknowledgment." "After we survive," Keating replied. "Heroes can wait for credits."

Monash's voice, sharp and immediate:

"Prime Minister, boats are fifteen minutes out. Request weapons free authorization."

"Michael, wait one." She turned back to Reid. "You're right about Article IV. It's a trap. But you're wrong about Australia. We don't need America to save us. We don't need Beijing to stabilize us. We just need to last longer than your plan."

She picked up the handset, speaking to Monash but watching Reid. "General, you are authorized to defend Australian territory with all necessary force. Repel boarders. Protect the beaches. But Michael—no declarations, no attributions. This is not war. This is pest control."

Reid's smile finally died. "You can't—"

"I can. I am. We're not invoking Article IV. We're not declaring war. We're just going to defend ourselves, quietly, competently, without giving your architects the excuse they need."

"People will die!"

"People have been dying. In hospitals without power. In aged care without cooling. Your network killed them as surely as bullets." She turned to the AFP officers. "Take him back. Charge him with treason. Let the courts decide if we're at war."

As they led Reid out, he turned at the door. "The boats will keep coming. Tonight, tomorrow, next week. How long can you defend without declaring?"

"Longer than your money lasts."

The door closed. Keating turned back to the display where the boats were now ten minutes from Australian sand. Through the southern window, communications flowed clear for the first time in hours. She could hear everything—NORFORCE teams reporting positions, RBS-70 operators confirming targets, Monash coordinating the defense with the quiet competence of someone who'd prepared for this moment without wanting it.

"Prime Minister," Vale said softly. "If those boats land—"

"They won't."

"But if they do—"

"Then we deal with that reality when it arrives. But we don't hand them the war they're trying to manufacture."

Her phone buzzed. Sophie from Sydney: *Crowds dispersing. Music worked again. Holding the city with Midnight Oil and news. Whatever's happening up north, we're steady here.*

Keating typed back: *Beach defense imminent. No war declarations. Just Australians being stubborn.*

On the display, the boats crossed into Australian territorial waters. Twelve nautical miles. Clear violation.

"Warning shots authorized," Monash's voice came through clear. "NORFORCE teams, light them up."

Tracer fire erupted from the dunes—beautiful and terrible, drawing lines between sand and sea. The lead boat stuttered, slowed. The formation behind began to scatter.

"They're not stopping," someone reported.

Keating lifted the handset for national broadcast. The red light came on immediately—they'd been waiting.

"This is the Prime Minister. In a few minutes, hostile vessels will attempt to land on Australian beaches. Our forces will stop them. This is not a declaration of war. This is Australians defending Australia. We know who sent them, even if we can't prove it in court. We know what they want—chaos, escalation, an excuse to intervene. We're not giving it to them."

Through the window, Canberra's night stretched peaceful and deceptive. Somewhere, her daughter was listening to this broadcast. Somewhere, Reid's architects were realizing their script had been rejected.

"We will defend every beach, every city, every piece of infrastructure—not with declarations but with decisions. One boat, one system, one hour at a time. This is what we do. This is who we are."

On the display, the first boat hit the beach at Snake Bay.

And Australians were waiting.

CHAPTER 23: HOUR 22:00
SNAKE BAY

Major General Michael Monash

The first boat hit the sand at Snake Bay with the sound of fiberglass meeting Australia—harsh, sudden, irreversible. Through the night vision feeds, Monash watched eight figures leap into the shallows, weapons raised, moving with the practiced coordination of people who'd rehearsed this moment.

"Contact front," Shark Three reported, voice steady as stone. "Eight dismounted, moving to establish beachhead. Second boat coming in hot, third and fourth holding offshore."

The ops floor at JTF North had compressed to essential personnel—everyone else evacuated to secondary positions. On the main screen, infrared feeds from NORFORCE positions showed the beach in ghostly green. The boats appeared as white scars against dark water. The figures moving up the sand looked like every nightmare Monash had trained for but hoped would stay theoretical.

"Warning shots," he ordered. "Make them reconsider."

Tracer fire erupted from the dunes—two bursts, deliberately high, drawing phosphorescent lines between the landing party and wherever they thought they were going. The figures dropped, took cover behind their boat, but didn't retreat.

"Sir," Julia Ng said, "they're deploying something from the boat."

On screen, two of the figures were hauling equipment onto the sand. Not weapons—communications gear. They were establishing a command node, claiming the beach not with flags but with bandwidth.

"They're validating the landing," the intelligence officer said. "Broadcasting success to justify what comes next."

Through the southern window—the laser link through space that had finally given them clear communications—Keating's voice cut through: "Michael, status?"

"Eight on the beach, more incoming. They're establishing position, not attacking. This is theater."

"Then close the curtain."

"Rules of engagement?"

"Minimum force for maximum effect. Detain if possible, repel if necessary. No casualties if avoidable."

"Copy."

He turned to the room. "NORFORCE, advance to contact. Disrupt their equipment first, personnel second. RBS-70 teams, if anything launches from those boats, introduce it to gravity."

On screen, Shark Three's team materialized from the landscape—six Indigenous soldiers who knew this beach the way the intruders knew their rehearsals. They moved through the scrub with an economy that looked like the land itself had decided to object.

The first contact was brief. Flash-bangs erupted around the communications node. The landing party returned fire—disciplined bursts that said military training—but they were shooting at shadows that had already moved.

"Second boat beaching," Hargreaves called. "Third and fourth approaching."

"Light the water," Monash ordered.

Illumination rounds burst overhead, turning night into harsh sodium day. The boats stood exposed—military ribs with no markings, crews in tactical gear with no flags, the kind of deniable force that could be anyone or no one.

Through the feeds, he watched Shark Three's team flow around the landing party's flanks. No heroics, just practiced violence applied precisely. One intruder down with a bean bag round. Another tangled in wire that hadn't been there seconds ago. The communications node took a 40mm foam baton round and became expensive junk.

"Boats three and four breaking off," Julia reported. "They're withdrawing."

"No. They're repositioning. Track them."

The first landing party was falling back to their boat, dragging equipment and wounded pride. But they'd achieved something—they'd put boots on Australian sand. In Reid's script, that would justify everything that followed.

Except.

"Sir," Noah Tan appeared at Monash's shoulder, still breathless from his run from the evidence lockup. "The pattern—they want you to kill someone. Look."

He spread photos across the desk—images from the captured devices, the safehouses, the interrogations. "Every escalation has been designed to force lethal response. The infrastructure attacks, the crowds, now this. They need Australian forces to kill someone on camera to justify intervention."

Monash looked at the screen where the landing party was trying to refloat their boat while NORFORCE harried them with non-lethal rounds and aggressive disapproval.

"All stations," he said into the net, "weapons discipline absolute. We disable and detain. No deadly force unless Australian lives in immediate danger. Make them fail boring."

The second boat was trying to extract the first. Someone on boat three was pointing what looked like a weapon—

"SAM launch from boat three!" Hargreaves shouted.

The missile streaked up, locked onto something, veered toward the Wedgetail orbiting thirty thousand feet above.

"Countermeasures," Monash ordered, though the E-7 crew was already responding.

Chaff bloomed. The missile corkscrewed, confused, found nothing, self-destructed in frustrated puffs.

"That's attempted murder of ADF personnel," Julia said.

"That's exactly what they want us to call it," Monash replied. "Wedgetail, you intact?"

"Slightly insulted but operational," came the controller's voice. "We're tracking launcher position."

"Mark it but don't prosecute. Boats three and four, give them something to think about."

The RAN patrol boat Cape Byron had crept within range during the chaos. Her 25mm Typhoon mount spoke once—a burst across the bow of boat three that said clearly: we see you, we can touch you, decide wisely.

Boats three and four decided wisely. They turned north, engines screaming, running for international waters.

On the beach, the first landing party had a choice—stand and fight while outnumbered, or retreat and declare victory for touching Australian soil.

They chose retreat, badly. The boat's engine caught Australian disapproval in the form of a 40mm foam baton that turned the outboard into abstract art. They were going nowhere.

"Shark Three, secure and detain."

"With pleasure."

What followed was less battle than aggressive arrest. NORFORCE swept the beach with the practiced efficiency of people who'd been preparing for this since their grandfathers' time. Eight intruders face-down in sand, zip-tied, equipment scattered and catalogued.

"Sir," the intelligence officer said, studying the captured gear, "no identification, no markings, but... the weapons are Chinese Type 95s. The comms are Russian. The boats are Iranian copies of US designs."

"Deliberately mixed to prevent attribution."

"Or to implicate everyone."

Through the southern window, Keating's voice: "Michael?"

"Eight detained, no casualties our side, minor injuries theirs. Boats one and two captured, three and four withdrew. We have prisoners and equipment but no flags."

"Can we prove state action?"

"We can prove someone wanted us to think it was state action."

A pause. Then: "Good enough for tonight. Well done."

The connection held—clear for the first time all day through the laser link bouncing off satellites that didn't care about politics. Monash thought about the technology, about the fact that they'd had this capability all along but saved it until desperate. Sometimes the best weapon was the one you didn't use until you had to.

"Sir," Noah said, flipping through his binder, "based on the pattern, they'll try one more escalation before midnight.

Something that forces Article IV."

"What's left?"

"Something we can't ignore. Mass casualty, critical infrastructure, or—" He stopped, staring at a notation he'd made hours ago. "The water supply. We've protected power, communications, fuel. But the water treatment plants—"

Monash looked at the clock: 22:34. Eighty-six minutes until Day Zero became Day One.

"Julia, flash to all units. Water infrastructure goes to maximum security now. If someone wants to poison Darwin, they're running out of time to try."

On the beach, NORFORCE was photographing everything—every piece of equipment, every pocket's contents, every serial number that might exist. Building the legal case that would matter when the world asked what happened.

The detained intruders sat in a line, faces covered, hands secured. Someone's satellite was undoubtedly watching, recording Australian forces processing prisoners with careful adherence to laws the other side had already abandoned.

"Sir," Hargreaves said, "boats three and four have crossed into international waters. They're being recovered by a larger vessel. No markings."

"Track it until it becomes someone else's problem."

Monash looked at the map—Darwin still dark by design, the beaches secured, the infrastructure defended. They'd won the hour. But Reid's script had more pages, and the night wasn't over.

"All stations," he said, "prepare for final surge. They have eighty minutes to force us into war. We have eighty minutes to disappoint them."

Through the window, Darwin's selective darkness stretched

toward a horizon that didn't care about human timelines. Somewhere, Keating was preparing another broadcast. Somewhere, Reyes was keeping the city's heartbeat steady with atomic clocks and stubbornness. Somewhere, Sophie was explaining to five million people why gunfire on beaches didn't mean war.

The coin in his pocket sat heavy and unspent. His father had carried it through three tours without knowing if he was winning or losing, just knowing he was still there.

"Rotate crews at 22:45," Monash ordered. "Fresh eyes for the last hour. Whatever they're planning for midnight, we meet it awake."

On the screen, the beach at Snake Bay looked peaceful again—just sand and scrub and the eternal argument between land and sea. But the boot prints remained, evidence that someone had tried to change the definition of Australian territory.

They'd failed.

For now.

CHAPTER 24: HOUR 23:00
DAY ONE

Prime Minister Patricia Keating

The Article IV envelope sat unopened on the table like an accusation she'd refused to hear. Twenty-three hours since the first cable cut, and Patricia Keating hadn't touched it once. Through the submarine room's speakers, she could hear Sydney coming back online—substations clearing, crowds becoming neighbors again, the particular sound of infrastructure remembering how to breathe.

The Article IV envelope sat unopened on the table like an accusation she'd refused to hear. Twenty-three hours since the first cable cut, and Patricia Keating hadn't touched it once. Through the submarine room's speakers, she could hear Sydney coming back online—substations clearing, crowds becoming neighbors again, the particular sound of infrastructure remembering how to breathe.

"Southern window remains stable," Vale said, entering with coffee that had given up pretending. "Woomera reports the laser path is burning clear. We can maintain sovereign communications indefinitely."

Keating turned from the wall display where Darwin still showed its deliberate darkness, the hospital's green square the only constant through the entire crisis. "Reid?"

"Processed. Charged. His network's being rolled up across three states." Vale set down fresh numbers. "Seventeen arrests in Sydney, twelve in Melbourne, eight in Brisbane. The parliamentary passes alone will take weeks to trace."

Through the speaker, AM radio carried Sophie Kerr's voice from Sydney: steady, exhausted, still telling five million people what came next. The woman had become Australia's nightlight—constant, unfancy, necessary.

"NATO's Article Five?" Keating asked.

"Ratified. But the Americans can't project. Their grid's worse than ours—Reid was right about that much."

Keating picked up the red pen she'd carried since her first Cabinet meeting, turned it once. "He was wrong about the rest. We didn't need Article Four. We didn't need to name an enemy. We just needed to last."

Her phone showed a text from her daughter: *Power's back in the residence. We're making tea for everyone. Proper tea, in cups, like civilization.*

She typed back: *That's how we win.*

The secure line rang—clear through the southern window. "Prime Minister? General Monash."

"Michael. Status?"

"Detainees processed. Beach secured. Water infrastructure checked clean. Darwin's ready to restore when Reyes gives the word."

"You made the right decisions. All of them."

A pause. "Thank you, ma'am."

She hung up and looked at the envelope again. The paper inside that would have changed everything, committed them to a war they couldn't define against an enemy they couldn't legally name. Reid had been so certain she'd open it.

"Burn it," she told Vale.

"Prime Minister?"

"The envelope. Have it destroyed. Witnessed. We never opened it, so we never invoked it. Let the lawyers argue about what that means."

Vale took the envelope carefully, like handling evidence of a crime prevented. As she reached the door, Keating added: "And Vale? Schedule Cabinet for 0700. Full restore. We've got a country to rebuild and we're doing it without declaring war on anyone."

Major General Michael Monash

The ops floor had found its second wind, or maybe its fifth. Twenty-three hours of crisis had worn grooves in the watchstanders' routines—coffee at this angle, notes in that corner, the specific lean that meant someone was fighting sleep and winning.

Monash stood behind Julia Ng's station, finally allowing himself to see the whole picture. Darwin dark but breathing. Beaches secured. Eight detainees whose interrogation would take months but whose failure had taken minutes. The coin in his pocket—his father's, from Vietnam—sat heavy and unspent.

"Fuel depot's asking about restoration timeline," Ng said, one hand still on her keyboard while the other held a phone that hadn't stopped ringing. "Havel wants to know if he can start pumping the sacrificial pit."

"Tell him ecological recovery comes after infrastructure recovery. The frogs can write letters next week."

She almost smiled—first time in twenty-three hours. Around them, the ops floor was transitioning from crisis to sustained operations. The adrenaline leaving, the exhaustion arriving, the particular satisfaction of having held when everything said break.

"Sir," Hargreaves called from radar, "Cape Byron reports the recovery vessel has disappeared into international waters. No identification possible."

"They'll be back," Monash said. "Different boats, same intent."

"But not tonight."

"No. Not tonight."

He pulled out the coin finally, let it roll across his knuckles once. His father had carried it through three tours, '68 to '71, never spent it, never explained it. Michael understood now. Some currency wasn't for spending. It was for remembering you still had choices, even when all the choices looked impossible.

"Sir?" Ng held up a secure phone. "Prime Minister."

He'd already spoken to Keating, but this was different. This was the formal call, the one that went in records.

"Michael," her voice carried the weight of decision. "For the record: your unilateral elevation to full defensive posture, your authorization of force to repel boarders, your decision to neutralize maritime threats—all are retroactively approved under emergency command provisions."

"Thank you, Prime Minister."

"Don't thank me. You held Darwin with copper wire and determination while I sat in Canberra arguing about punctuation. The country owes you more than approval."

After she hung up, he stood for a moment in the quiet efficiency of his ops floor. These people—Ng, Hargreaves, the nameless specialists who'd translated chaos into comprehension—they'd held the line without knowing if anyone would thank them or blame them.

"All stations," he said into the net. "Stand down to sustained operations. Maintain beach patrols. Coordinate with Lieutenant Reyes for restoration sequence. Get some food that doesn't lie about being food. And people—" He paused, looked at each tired face. "You did good."

No speeches. They weren't the type. But Ng's fingers stopped moving for just a second, and Hargreaves actually looked up from his scope, and that was enough.

The coin went back in his pocket, unspent. Some currency you kept to remind you why the spending mattered.

Through the southern window—that commercial gift they'd never asked for but gratefully used—a final report arrived from Woomera. The connection would hold as long as needed. The oligarchs had their uses.

Lieutenant Kailana Reyes

The rubidium clock hummed its atomic truth while Darwin waited in engineered darkness. Kailana Reyes stood at the master panel with both palms flat against the metal, feeling the city's potential through her fingertips. Twenty-three hours since the first cable bit, and she'd held Darwin together with physics and stubbornness.

"Southern window's stable," AEMO confirmed through the speaker. "Woomera says the time beacon's clean. You can trust the sync."

Trust. After a day of everything lying—timestamps, certificates, the very notion of "now"—she could finally trust something.

She opened the restoration sequence she'd been building for the last hour. Not the automatic cascade the system wanted, but careful, manual, suspicious. Every substation checked for cans. Every protection relay verified against atomic time. Every generator brought online like coaxing a frightened animal.

"Start with Nightcliff," she told the room. "Residential only. Let them make breakfast."

The first district came up clean. Lights in windows, the particular joy of electricity returning. Then Coconut Grove. Then Parap. Each success building on the last, the grid remembering how to be a grid.

Her phone buzzed. Unknown Sydney number: *This is Sophie. We're watching Darwin come back online. It's beautiful from here.*

She typed: *Just doing the job.*

No. You did more than that.

Another message, this one from a Darwin number she'd memorized without meaning to: *Rails neutralized cleanly. Good hands on both ends. —SC*

Sienna Crossman. The pilot who'd turned physics into poetry over Newcastle. They'd never met, might never meet, but they'd saved each other's infrastructure from opposite ends of the crisis.

"RDH requesting priority restore for admin wings," Patricia called out.

"Give them half. Keep NICU and ICU on generators until we're certain." Reyes pulled up the hospital's consumption curve. "Actually, leave NICU on backup for another hour. Those machines don't forgive surprises."

The city came back in pieces. Not the automatic flood of normal restoration, but careful, considered, suspicious. Each district tested before trusting. Each connection verified against their own atomic noon.

"Berrimah substation's asking about the industrial sector."

"Tomorrow. Heavy industry waits until we've swept every cabinet twice."

She thought about the devices they'd pulled—forty-three magnetic cans designed to make time lie. The sophistication of it. The patience. Someone had spent months preparing for this day, and she'd beaten them with a rubidium box from the F-18 shop and copper wire that remembered when digital was fiction.

The master panel showed Darwin at sixty percent restoration. The hospital square pulsed perfect green. Base power steady. The desal plant had stopped sulking and started working.

"That's enough for tonight," she announced. "Rest stays dark until dawn. Let people sleep."

She pulled her palms from the panel finally. Twenty-three hours of feeling the city's pulse through metal and decisions. Her hands tingled with absence.

Outside, Darwin's selective light painted new constellations. Not the full blaze of normal night, but enough. Enough to say they'd held. Enough to say they'd won this round.

The rubidium clock hummed on, one pulse per second, honest and indifferent.

They were their own noon. And noon had held.

Flight Lieutenant Sienna Crossman

The F-35 sat in its hardstand like a sleeping predator, skin still warm from the evening sortie. Sienna walked around it once—habit, ritual, respect. Twenty-three hours since first scramble, four sorties, every weapon delivered exactly where intended. The jet had done its job without complaint.

"Maintenance wants her for twelve hours," the crew chief said, appearing with a clipboard that had seen better decades. "Full diagnostic after that rail strike."

"She earned it."

Through the hangar doors, she could see Williamtown transitioning from combat tempo to sustained readiness. Pilots landing, crews rotating, the particular exhaustion of victory without declaration.

Her phone showed messages she hadn't read—coordination updates, fuel status, a dozen things that mattered six hours ago. One stood out, Darwin number: *Grid restoration beginning. Your precision gave us time. Thank you. —KR*

Kailana Reyes. The engineer she'd never met who'd held Darwin's infrastructure with atomic clocks and determination while Sienna cleared the skies. They'd saved each other without introduction.

"Ma'am?" Nikki Parnell appeared, still in her flight suit, helmet under arm. "Debrief in ten. Intel wants everything about the rails."

"They were exactly where they were supposed to be. We put ordnance exactly where it was supposed to go. Physics met physics."

"You know they want more than that."

"Then they can want. The job got done clean."

She looked north toward where Unknown-12 was probably being stripped in international waters, its mission as dead as its crane. No attribution, no headlines, just steel bent beyond utility. Tomorrow there would be another boat, another probe. But tonight, the sea was quiet.

Sophie Kerr

The newsroom had the particular quiet of exhaustion earning its rest. Half the monitors were dark—power-saving or simply given up. The AM chain still hummed, that beautiful analog signal from Prospect that had carried five million people through the darkness.

Sophie sat at her desk with the emergency mic close enough to grab if needed. Through the window, Sydney's CBD showed its recovery in patches—building lights returning in careful sequence, street lamps remembering their job, the electric skeleton rebuilding itself.

"That's the last of them," Mo said, appearing with two cups of something claiming to be coffee. "Mascot substation's clear. Marrickville's restored. The Farnham Protocol stands down."

She took the coffee, didn't drink it. Twenty-three hours of talking, and she'd found the rhythm—not news anchor, not crisis manager, just a voice in the dark saying "we're still here" until it was true.

Her phone showed a text from the Prime Minister herself: *Thank you for holding Sydney steady. Your voice mattered more than you know.*

She typed back: *Just did what the old AM transmitter was built for. Being there when everything else fails.*

On her desk, the notebook where she'd tracked the comma tell sat open. Twelve languages, same error, perfect tracking signature. Tomorrow the intelligence services would dissect it, trace it, build legal cases from punctuation. Tonight it was just evidence that someone had tried to break Australia with grammar and failed.

"Sophie?" Linh appeared, tablet clutched like always. "Keating's doing final broadcast in ten. Want to carry it?"

"Of course."

She pulled on the headphones one more time. Through the window, Sydney was learning how to be electric again. Not the full bright of before, but careful, conscious consumption. The city had learned something in the dark.

Red light on.

"This is ABC Sydney. Sophie Kerr with you as we head toward

midnight. If you're just joining us after power restoration, welcome back. We held the darkness together, and now we're sharing the light the same way."

Midnight crept across Australia without ceremony. Day Zero became Day One in the small spaces—digital clocks resetting, generators winding down, the particular relief of systems returning to baseline.

But in Canberra, a folder marked CABINET ONLY described infrastructure vulnerabilities that ran deeper than cables. In Darwin, interrogation rooms held eight people whose silence cost more than their words. In Sydney, the comma tell had become a meme, but the network that created it was still being mapped. And sixty nautical miles northeast of Darwin, dark water held no boats but remembered their intent.

Patricia Keating stood at her window watching Canberra pretend toward normal while knowing the pretense was all they had. Tomorrow would bring questions—attribution, retaliation, the slow work of courts and evidence. But tonight, Australia had refused to declare a war it couldn't define against an enemy it couldn't name. Sometimes the victory was in what you didn't do.

Michael Monash left the ops floor to younger watches, the coin in his pocket still unspent. His father would have understood—some fights you won by refusing to make them bigger than they were.

Kailana Reyes finally let Darwin's grid run itself, trusting automation now that time had agreed to be honest. She'd held a city together with copper wire and atomic truth. Tomorrow there would be reports, investigations, probably a medal she'd never wear. Tonight, she just wanted to sleep.

In Sydney, Sophie Kerr watched the city rebuild its electric confidence one substation at a time. The AM transmitter out at Prospect would keep running—just in case, just because, just as witness that analog endurance outlasted digital sophistication.

The country exhaled once and found it was still there. Changed but not broken. Tested but not declared. The infrastructure could be rebuilt. The trust between neighbors during blackouts—that was harder to measure but impossible to destroy.

Somewhere, Reid's architects were recalculating. The probe had failed. Australia hadn't taken the bait. The region would reorganize, but not tonight, not through this crisis.

The long road to the Hardlands had begun—that space between what was and what would be, where old alliances meant less than new realities and infrastructure mattered more than ideology. Australia would walk it without declarations, one decision at a time, suspicious of timestamps but trusting atomic clocks.

This was not an ending. It was a translation—crisis becoming condition, emergency becoming normal, the first twenty-four hours of however long the new world would take to arrive.

The war that wasn't a war would continue tomorrow.

Australia would continue back.

THE END

ABOUT THE AUTHOR

Climate change and the theory that greenhouse gases are driving rapid temperature increases were not designed by radical activists seeking to overturn capitalism and the industrial miliary complex.

Joss G. Hamilton writes speculative fiction that explores how ordinary people navigate extraordinary change, with particular interest in how middle-power nations like Australia adapt to shifting global dynamics. His work bridges technical authenticity with human drama, creating stories that feel both immediate and universal.

The *Hardlands* universe, of which *Severance* serves as the opening salvo, examines a world where traditional alliances shift and smaller nations must chart independent courses through increasingly complex international waters. Hamilton's approach combines meticulous research into military and technical procedures with deep respect for the professionals who keep civilization running during crisis.

Severance, written in radio-play style and inspired by classic dramatic broadcasts, represents Hamilton's vision of crisis as catalyst—twenty-four hours that reveal character, test institutions, and force nations to choose what they truly value. The novella draws from influences ranging from *War of the Worlds* to the television series *24*, while maintaining distinctly Australian perspectives on resilience and response.

Behind the pen name stands a storyteller committed to proving that the most compelling dramas unfold not in capitals of empire, but in the spaces between—where competent people make impossible choices with whatever tools they have available.

Joss lives in Australia with his family, surrounded by the landscapes and communities that continue to inspire stories of quiet strength in uncertain times. *Severance* is his third published work and the first entry in the *Hardlands* universe.

www.ingramcontent.com/pod-product-compliance
Lightning Source LLC
LaVergne TN
LVHW091149080826
845145LV00008B/2313